SUPERTANKER
PORT OF CALL ASIA

BY

WILLIAM GILBERT

Book cover design by The Scarlett Rugers Design Agency
www.scarlettrugers.com

Captain Thompson looked out from the wrought iron balcony and upon the vista of the port, shimmering in the heat. The sweat soaked his clothes, but the worn out fan just inside the open doorway managed to cool his back just enough to make his shirt irritatingly clammy. Out there was his ship, worn out too, just like the fan, thought Thompson. Thompson did not get the nice new tankers. It took, tough, belligerent, old school captains like him to keep the worn out wrecks moving. The young, smart, captains with their procedures and their documentation were given the new tankers because they were the only ones with which they could cope. Life was not fair. Thompson saw himself as taking his own life bit by bit to Bangladeshi scrapyards.

How many thousands of miles had he sailed. How many circumnavigations had he made. How many suns had he sighted. How many noon positions had he put on charts.

He raised himself up to look down at the pavement and at some young girls walking past. Sadness overwhelmed him and then he was all right again. His wife had left him and his mind was turning things over. His daughter had gone. It was open for him to go with young girls now. He didn't think, I've got a daughter your age, and feel the guilt.

He'd despised all those seamen who threw themselves on any young girls working in the dives to which they went after a day swinging derricks and scrubbing and painting and now, after all these years, he found himself inclined to join them.

The mama-san was behind him. The sailors had enjoyed watching him slope off with her no doubt. Well, he didn't care anymore. I paid my dues, he thought. I tried to be what society wanted me to be.

Long arms were draped over his chest. All those years, he thought. All those years of listening to his wife and supplying her with whatever she wanted and listening to his failings listed, over and over again, and it all added up to nothing.

The ship was laid up but Thompson still felt obliged to put in a daily appearance. He could probably get away without doing it. After all his years with the company would they care, but he clung on to a smidgen of professional pride.

Thompson was jostled in the street outside and his hand flew to his breast pocket to check his wallet was still there and then he climbed inside a smoking yellow taxi and went off to work.

The mama-san looked out at him from the balcony windows as he left, shrewdly evaluating her client and then turned and went back inside.

At the jail, the radio officer was being questioned. He had little idea of what had happened to him and was floundering. They laughed when he said he wanted to see the British consul. "Where do you think you are?" said the sergeant The radio officer wiped the blood from his eyes. "Stop scratching," said the sergeant. "You reopened the wound."

"I wasn't scratching," said the radio officer grumpily.

"She says you owe her money," said the sergeant.

"I don't owe her any money," said the radio officer. "Listen, why would I rip her off?"

"I don't listen," said the sergeant, "you listen." The radio officer sighed. Through the glass partition, he could see the girl gesticulating in front of a corporal. Oh God, he thought. Just imagine if she starts sobbing. Five years in jail for a whitey like him, twenty to a cell. He was aware that the sergeant was speaking to him again. "Maybe we can help you to negotiate," he said.

"Negotiate what. I don't owe her anything?" said the radio officer with exasperation.

"You admit that you can't remember, so how can you be sure," said the sergeant. "You have a bad attitude. I am trying to help you."

"Some help. Just tell her to leave me alone."

"In this country," said the sergeant pompously, " we respect women." The radio officer laughed, and the sergeant leaned forward and slapped him, opening the cut more.

The radio officer said, "I won't pay." He looked smugly at the sergeant. "That's a problem for you isn't it. You'd like to avoid any complications, but you want the money. If you were to call the British consul, he would lean on me but you won't call him." The sergeant glared at him.

"We will take the money out of your wallet. What will you do about that?" he asked him. The radio officer shrugged with an exaggerated movement.

"There's probably about five dollars in it," he said.

"And your Rolex," said the sergeant.

"It's a fake," said the radio officer. The sergeant glared at him again.

"You will get into trouble with your company," he said.

"They really couldn't care less," said the radio officer. "If you throw me in jail for the next ten years, they won't be in the slightest bit bothered. The ship's not going anywhere for a while. It's laid up. They don't even need a radio officer. They just can't be bothered to organise a flight home."

The sergeant wasn't used to this intransigence. He tried his last weapon. "Your wife," he said.

"Left me years ago," replied the radio officer.

The sergeant looked annoyed. He flicked his eyes up at his men and nodded at the exit and they picked up the radio officer and more or less threw him out into the bright sunlight. He stood there among the tuk-tuks and the pedestrians and smiled. Sometimes a man who didn't care anymore had a huge advantage in life.

Thompson sat in his office struggling with the huge typewriter. The company had wanted to give him a computer, but he fought it. "I don't want one," he said. "They ruined the cargo trade. Without them we'd never have had containerisation."

There wasn't much to do. He chased up the engineers. He mourned his daughter. He cursed his wife for being a bitch. Ex-wife, he thought to himself. He was surviving without her but not particularly well. As punishment for having supported her for thirty years, the courts were demanding that he support her for another thirty.

The radio officer entered the ship's office. He looked a little the worse for wear. "Been at the police station," he said.

"Cost you?" asked Thompson.

"Nah," said the radio officer, "I wouldn't pay any supposed fine." Thompson raised his eyebrows.

"That's either brave or stupid," he said. The radio officer shrugged. "Watch your step now," Thompson told him. "You've brought shame on whichever sergeant was responsible for this and the only way he can get rid of that is to make you pay."

"I'll be careful," said the radio officer. "Maybe I'll go home."

"That is a good idea," said Thompson, emphatically.

Maggie sat with her pet boy in Wong's, her whore bar. Her face sometimes looked a little chiselled and her habit of slapping and biting her companions when drunk led some to speculate that she was a lady boy and then the next moment she would fling a leg up so high that it was almost vertical and put it on a man's shoulder and announce that she had been a dancer with the Chinese national ballet a long time ago and they would think, hmmm, maybe not.

Maggie was looking for love. Before Deng Xioaping ruined things for her by bringing success and privilege to so many and leading her to be cast out in the sudden influx of competition, she had been on top. There were rumours that she had been the mistress of a very senior party official.

She owned Wong's but was not so stupid as to have her name on any paperwork. She was perturbed at the moment. That English crew had come in and then she had lost them to her rival's establishment and her spies told her that the captain himself had gone home with the mama-san. This had caused her a great loss of face. She had beaten one of her girls and then fired her in her fury, only to take the sobbing teenager back a few hours later when she came in, begging her for mercy as, if she were fired, she would bring so much shame upon her family. Maggie had looked at her cooly and thought the father will beat her for bringing the shame onto the family but will be thinking only of the lost money. "Do not worry," she had said. "I will not force your lazy father to struggle for the money to buy his opium and have to think about substituting betel nut. I curse myself for being so kind-hearted."

She sent some subliminal signal to her pet boy and he rose and brought her a fresh glass of wine. The captain was hers, she thought. He was lonely and vulnerable. And the rest of the crew were to have their pockets emptied on a nightly basis by her girls.

She knew about the incident with the radio officer. In fact, she had organised it. He should know better than to chase freelancers. This could only help her. She had told them all that they were safe in her establishment and they had moved on anyway. She considered having the sergeant rearrest the radio officer just to drive her point home but the sergeant probably couldn't be bothered even if she paid him some more.

The radio officer's girl appeared in the doorway and Maggie flicked her eyes to the chair at her side. She sat down and looked dutiful. "You did well," said Maggie. "Just enough to frighten them. They will be here for a long time and there's about twenty or thirty thousand passing through their hands every month." The girl exhaled.

"I was so afraid that you would be angry because the sergeant did not jail him for longer."

Maggie smiled and put her arm around the girl's shoulder.

"The sergeant is lazy," she said. "In any case, I wanted them frightened, not terrified." She sipped her glass of wine. "You may leave now," she said. The girl scurried out.

Thompson moaned to the chief engineer which was a waste of time as the chief engineer was old school and had spent thirty years working in engine rooms without ear defenders and was more or less completely deaf. He nodded understandingly as Thompson ranted. Even though he didn't hear the words he knew the substance. It was the same rant that captains shouted in the ears of their engineers down engine rooms all over the world.

"This is the second time they've done this to me," Thompson was saying. "Bloody Terry," he said. The chief turned to look at him. Thompson looked puzzled. "Bloody Terry," he said. The chief engineer lip read the word Terry and nodded.

"Aye," he said. Thompson looked at him as if unsure that he really understood and then decided he did and went off on his rant again. Eventually, the chief engineer sighed and moved away towards the control room. Thompson frowned and went back up the steel stairway and out onto the deck.

The third mate was there, hanging over the rails. "Can't you find something to do?" he said to him angrily. The third mate looked miffed and sidled off towards the main deck.

I could have been retired by now, Thompson thought, if it hadn't been for that bitch. Why the hell did I ever get married. Why did I have a kid. I never even saw her and then she killed herself. Why did I ever go to sea. He booted the bulwark with his steel toe-capped safety shoe. Damn, he said. Suddenly, he noticed that he was not wearing his watch. He grimaced and then sighed. Bloody mama-san, he said.

The mam-san looked at Thompson's watch lying on her window sill. What a stupid man to take it off. Was that going to make their love-making any more real. She examined it carefully in the light from the window. Swiss but not extravagantly expensive. She would give it back to him and go for the long haul. Thompson was single and lonely and here for months. She would get far more out of him than the value of this watch.

When she arrived at her place, it was closed and dusty and just looked seedy in the low light through the blinds. She yelled out for her boy and he came running from the kitchen. "Why haven't you cleaned up yet?" she demanded. He went on for too long with some lame excuse and she gave up listening.

She thought of doing something with the decorations. The signed photograph of the U.S. naval ship had seemed to annoy the British tanker crew for some reason. She had thought they were allies. But the British had got on great with the Russian sailors who had been in. Customers were so confusing. Just take their money, she thought.

All this had been paid for by a boyfriend, a Dutch seaman. He had fallen in love with her, taken her to Holland, which she had hated, decided that he didn't really want an Asian wife, and given her a lot of money to go home again which was what she had done with glee. She had returned like a retired French prostitute of the nineteenth century going home to the provinces a substantial woman after years of flinging herself on her back for the beau monde, to the respect of her community.

She sat down and twirled Thompson's watch around in the dust on a dimly lit table. Perhaps it was time to do the same again. A new injection of money would not go amiss. The place needed doing up. She was tired of old men but the old men had the money and they were more ready to settle for a few moments of scuffling under the blankets and then the mature conversation which she was so practised in offering.

The chief engineer stared at the panels in the control room and took a swig from his flask. "No alcohol," he said to himself, scornfully, thinking of the company's new policy, introduced to keep the insurance company happy. "Fire me if you don't like it." Then he adopted his normal preoccupied expression again. This was it for him. Home, school, Clyde shipyard apprenticeship, merchant navy, old age. It had all passed by him without his seeming to even notice. He focussed on a red pen holder. It was an exercise he tried sometimes. He had never really understood what people meant by meditation but that was what he was attempting to do now, clear his mind and focus on an object. His contempt for non-conformists would have led him to be horrified if it ever became apparent to him that he was indulging in something related to hippies and their like much as if a rabid homophobe's latent homosexuality suddenly revealed itself in his consciousness.

The whisky tasted great. It was the last of the good stuff from duty-free and now he would have to drink the cheap stuff the Filipinos smuggled on board or go out and buy some.

His son wanted to go to sea and he was despairing about this. He tried to find words to express his objections, but, when confronted with him, he just found himself falling silent and smiling at him in embarrassment. The spiky hair and fashionable clothes intimidated him a bit. He knew his son regarded him as nothing more than an occasional nuisance, appearing at random times in the family home for a few months or maybe even less, and then disappearing again, and thought he didn't love him or care about him and the chief had no idea how to tell him that he did. His son would say, if he told him, that he didn't want him to go to sea, that he hadn't spoken to him in sixteen years, what would make him think he was going to listen to him now. Or he would accuse him of having some ulterior motive.

His son was aggressive. The solitude and loneliness on ships would not turn him into a morose individual like himself; it would make him more violent. He thought of writing him a letter. "Don't do it boy. Believe me. I love you and all I want is for you to be happy and I don't think you will be if you follow in my footsteps." But he couldn't face the moment when they met again months later and they both knew the letter existed. Fifty-five years of emotional repression couldn't be overcome in five minutes. It probably couldn't be overcome at all.

Thompson opened the company mail. Ethical environmental policy, he read at the top of the first sheet which he pulled out of the biggest envelope. "Your hypocrisy knows no bounds," he muttered quietly. He became aware that the third mate was standing in the doorway. "What?" he said impatiently.

"I'd like to fly my girlfriend out," said the third mate shuffling his feet in embarrassment.

"Shields girl?" said Thompson with malice.

"Yeah, how did you know?" said the surprised third mate.

"Psychic," said Thompson, "and it's yes captain, not yeah." The third mate was intimidated. "Shields girls don't survive very long outside South Shields," said Thompson. "Did you even check that she has a passport?"

The third mate seemed even more embarrassed. "No," he answered. Thompson affected world-weariness.

"Tell me," he said, 'with all these Asian dolls around why you feel the need to fly a woman half way around the world. He thought some more and added, "at vast expense on your minimal salary."

"I don't sleep with whores, I have too much self-respect," said the boy. Thompson lowered his new reading glasses and looked at him over the top of them.

"Careful boy," he said.

"I don't mean you," stuttered the third mate. "I mean...," Thompson shifted his spectacles back into place.

"You're either an idiot or an admirable young man," he said. "I honestly don't know which. Yeah, go on, fly her out. She's not staying on board though. I don't want women on board," he paused for thought, "unless they definitely are hookers," he continued. The boy turned to go. "Just a minute," said Thompson and the boy turned to face him again. "When she gets here," he said, "you're going to get lots of invites to bring her out with other members of the crew. Don't do it even though you'll be proud of her and want to show her off. Just bring her once in the daytime, show her the ship, introduce her to everyone and send her back to her hotel."

"Why?" said the boy.

"Because they'll say more and more offensive things in a bid to get her to bite or to show that she's offended and give them what they'll consider to be a legitimate excuse to hate her and because she'll look at us and think that you'll probably turn out like us in some years' time. You will," he said, "but it's best that she doesn't realise that yet." The boy was looking at him as if he were a lunatic. "Dismissed," said Thompson lightly and fluttered his hand to indicate that the boy should leave him alone now. The boy went away, unsure whether to be elated or suicidal.

Maggie and her pet boy went for a walk down the street. Her boy held a parasol over her head to keep the sun off so that her skin would remain white and they took up the whole width of the pavement, but people respectfully stepped aside onto the road. She was well known in the community and people were a little bit frightened of her.

Outside the police station, the sergeant was climbing into his car. He turned to look at her and they both evaluated each other quietly and then Maggie and her pet boy continued their perambulations.

The other mama-san watched them from behind the thin curtains of her establishment. She envied Maggie her artistic pretensions. Along with the rest of the small town's population, she was uncertain as to the validity of Maggie's claims to have been a ballet dancer, but at least the thought of it was believable. No one would ever believe her to have been any sort of artiste.

They spilt the town and the sailors. It was a workable solution. The sailors liked to drift from one place to another. They didn't like it when they were confined to one establishment and when they loftily took offence at the attitude of some barmaid or prostitute in one joint they took great pride in adopting a superior manner and taking their business to the other. Both the mama-san and Maggie giggled at this behaviour even if they didn't like it.

In the dim interior of her place, the mama-san smoked a horrible smelling local cigarette and pondered the signed photograph of the U.S. navy destroyer sitting on the floor below the spot where it had been hanging. Best to keep it, she thought. Another U.S. navy ship might come in and it would make the American boys feel safe and at home if she were to put it back up.

Her boy was asleep in the back room. She rose and went to look at him lying on the silk sheets. This room she kept for them. No business took place here.

She pulled her top up and off and cast it aside and then took off her bra and sat down and peeled off her jeans and then flung her panties aside and climbed in beside him.

She was thirty and he was in his early twenties but this was a perk of the job.

He woke and rolled over and looked into her eyes. "You were tired," he said.

"Well, I'm not anymore," she replied. She reached out a hand and touched his cheek. "So beautiful," she said.

"That's what you pay me for," he said. She looked at him coolly.

"I don't pay you for that," she said, "I pay you for this," and she pulled him towards her.

The old fan in the ceiling in the main room slowly revolved squeaking once with every revolution and providing a kind of metronome sound on top of their moans.

Thompson wanted to speak to his wife. He hung out at the mission waiting for the Filipinos to leave the phone free for a moment and then dived in there. She answered quickly.

"Yes," she said and then more impatiently, "Who is this?"

"It's me," said Thompson.

"What do you want?" she said.

"You miss me?" he said.

"No, I don't," she told him. "Listen," she said. "It's over."

"Can't we still be friends?" said Thompson.

"You're fifty-eight," she said. "You're past being friends and you never had any friends anyway. You needed me, I needed you and now neither of us needs the other. Get on with your life. Find yourself some Asian girl like the rest of your kind." She was shrewd. She detected something in the delay in Thompson's reply. "You already have, haven't you?" she said. "Well, you know what, good for you." She seemed to be waiting for him to speak. "Now you're thinking that I won't take you back because of that but you're wrong because I never would have taken you back anyway. Can't we be honest after all these years. You don't even like me, and I don't even like you. We got married because everybody got married then. and we stayed married because we had a child, and we both... Well, she died and we don't have her anymore."

"O.K. O.K," said Thompson. "I won't bother you anymore." He went to hang up, but he heard her voice and rushed the receiver back to his ear.

"You were a good husband and a good father, despite what you think. It's just life that's all. You can still ring me if you like but not too often, O.K," she said.

"O.K.," said Thompson. He put the receiver back and leaned against the plastic screen and then realised that the Filipinos were waiting impatiently to get on it again, and he moved away to the bar and sat down and continued with his cheap beer.

Thompson sat on the beach with the mama-san and looked out at the sea. It was a lovely blue colour and the beach was beautiful with soft sand and just the odd piece of driftwood breaking up the solid yellow block of colour. He smoked a thin cheroot, a new pastime, and contemplated his existence. She reached up a hand and ran it down his upper arm and he smiled. "How long will you be here?" she said. He shrugged.

"You know I don't know," he said. "Let's just enjoy it while it lasts. I will anyway."

"Once I was married to a Dutchman," she said.

"Big blonde and handsome?" said Thompson. She giggled.

"Yes," she answered him. "But so Dutch. His sister hated me."

"Of course," said Thompson.

"You don't mind that you have to give me money?" she asked him.

"I'm too old to care," said Thompson, "and I'm not big, blonde or handsome." He wondered if he would burn, but his skin was not pale even though it wasn't tanned. He was just kind of ruddy.

"Do you like what you do? she asked him. He shrugged. "Do you even like the sea?" she persisted.

"I don't know," he said. "When I was a boy, I thought that it was a waste of a life to sit in an office and that I wanted adventure and travel and to be a man, and now I'm beginning to think that a lifetime of sitting in a little office and commuting and B and Q and Eastenders wouldn't have been so bad after all."

"You could live here like a king," she said.

"I might have been able to," he replied, "but she took everything."

"That's not right, you earnt it," she said.

"I see women's lib. will never take off here," he said.

"Tomorrow we can go somewhere else," she said. "My brother has a car."

"And see what?" he asked her.

"The country," she said. "You can't just lie on the beach and make love for the rest of your life."

"I could try," he said. "I could certainly try."

"You want to swim?" she said.

"I have an aversion to water," he told her. She raised her head and looked at him, her lips pursed. Then she stood up and took her bikini top off.

"How much longer are you going to have the opportunity to play in the surf with a half-naked woman?" she asked him.

Thompson reddened a little and then reddened more when he realised that he was reddening. He looked around to see if there were anyone else looking even though he didn't want to. Then he watched her running off into the sea and laughed and stood up and padded after her, his feet burning on the hot sand.

The sergeant stood outside his little jail and looked out at the bustle in the street. He was still infuriated by the uncooperative attitude of the radio officer. He knew better than to just hassle seamen and other foreigners for small offences and was kicking himself. If you were going to do it, you needed to get them for one of two offences because only over those two things would their consulates lose what little interest they actually had in being distracted from their whisky and their invitations and they were paedophilia and drugs.

His officers were laughing at him. His wife had already been told that he would be bringing her a nice present, and his girlfriend had been told that he would be bringing her an even nicer one. Now he didn't have the funds.

He stroked his moustache and fumed some more. He had been misled. That boy had looked softer than he actually was. Oh well, this was life. He would find some independent girl and sling her into the men's cage on the grounds that the women's was full and that would cheer him up. If it didn't, it would certainly cheer his officers up.

He saw Thompson across the street and cooly evaluated him. Tough guy or broken old man. Sometimes these old seamen flipped from one to the other. That man wouldn't care less if he were threatened with jail. He knew the type, fatalists.

He saw a group of the independent girls moving up the street. They would float through the bars that weren't strictly whore bars and pick up strays. They were fools to work without the protection of Maggie or the other mama-san. He identified his victim. She was fresh enough, just in from the country and still overwhelmed enough to be happy to just have sexy clothes and make up and not mind too much what she had to do for it.

His wife had looked like her once, before she grew fat. It had been strictly a business arrangement, marrying a local businessmen's daughter, but, for a while, he had been proud of her and then she had the first baby and gave up and what's more it wasn't even a son.

Two nuns walked past and he stepped out of their way. They gave him a nice smile. He made the little town safe. All the good citizens respected him. His daughter went to their school. She seemed very obedient to him so he never bothered to talk to her as he assumed she must be on the right path. In just a few years he would have to find her a husband. If anyone tried to pluck that flower before then, he would find that he disappeared off the face of the Earth.

Thompson walked off the flight at the provincial airport with a stoop which suggested he didn't want to be there. The humidity sapped his energy and he momentarily regretted coming, but he had felt a sense of duty.

He hung from the strap in the coach on the way to the little airport terminal and felt the badly adjusted air-conditioning chilling him.

The prison looked like a prisoner of war camp and Thompson looked around with disapproval as he went through the various security barriers. An Englishman really shouldn't be in here, he thought.

The visiting room was grim and Thompson sat in one of the cubicles and looked at the glass screen and waited patiently. The singsong chatter around him was piercing his brain and tiring him further. He longed to just stand up and scream, "Shut up," at them but the Empire was over and the natives were in charge.

Roly appeared in front of him and sat down. At least, he thought it was Roly. It was a very thin version of him. Roly picked up the telephone and Thompson looked to his side and saw that there was a receiver for him and picked his up.

"How you doing?" he said.

"Look like I've got cancer don't I," said Roly. Thompson shrugged. What's the point in lying, he thought.

"Yeah, you do," he said.

"I might," said Roly. "The prison's not got much of a hospital. I'd never find out even if I had. Did you hear anything about my wife? I don't get any mail, not that she'd bother writing."

"She's fine," said Thompson. Roly grimaced.

"The company still does business here after what they did to me?" he said.

"Yeah, they don't care," said Thompson.

"I could be here for years," said Roly. "The company's done nothing to get me out. The consul did nothing. The papers just think I'm a dolphin murderer 'caus of the spill. If I was pretty and had a pair of tits, the prime minister would personally petition the president."

"I thought I was always the bitter one," said Thompson.

"You were I suppose," said Roly.

"Not fair life is it?" said Thompson. "I've been a rotten bastard since forever, and you've always been a nice guy, and you're in here, and I'm not."

"The union was useless," said Roly.

"What do you expect for forty years of dues," said Thompson.

"I don't care anymore," said Roly. "I'd just as soon as die in here I suppose. I was never looking forward to retirement in any case. I suppose the Government would be happy if I just quietly died, the British Government I mean."

"They don't care Roly, because the media doesn't care. Like you say. You're not pretty and you don't have a pair of tits." Roly's head slumped. "I had a plastic bag full of cigarettes and stuff but the guards stole it," said Thompson sadly.

"They didn't steal it," said Roly. "I'll get it after they've sorted through it, then someone else will steal it."

"How many in a cell?" said Thompson.

"Twenty," said Roly. "It's not so bad though 'caus someone from our crew's got the word through that I've always been fair with them etc..,

"Typical," said Thompson. "The Government abandons you, the media abandons you, Terry throws you to the wolves, and yet the lowest paid, last people you'd think'd be interested, sort it."

"Yeah," said Roly. "They are reviewing my case again. It weren't my fault."

"Of course," said Thompson. The captain has all the responsibility and no authority. Is the British consulate keen to help."

"I already told you they weren't," said Roly tetchily. "I'm sorry," he said. "I didn't mean it like that. I'm grateful to you for coming."

"I understand," said Thompson. "No problems. Anything you want me to say to your sons. I'll be home in a few months."

"Nah," said Roly. "You know something, I never liked them anyway. They're all keen on this gap year thing but do you think they could fit this place into their itinerary so that they could visit me. Nah."

"Don't be bitter," said Thompson. If you have got cancer that'll only make it worse." He looked around. "That guard is saying this is over," he said. "I'd better go."

"Straight up north?" asked Roly.

"Oh, I've got someone to see first," said Thompson.

"Perhaps you could ask the consul how it's going?" said Roly. Thompson smiled.

"Oh I will," he said. "You can be sure I will. That's whom I've got to see." Roly shrugged and got up.

"Goodbye," he said. "Shame we can't shake hands."

"Don't give up," said Thompson.

"I suppose I won't," said Roly.

Thompson hammered on the apartment door. A smooth, public school, type in a silk dressing gown opened it, while a slinky looking ladyboy slid out of the living room behind him. "Do you know what time it is?" he demanded in a prissy superior voice." Thompson nodded.

"Yeah, I do." he said.

"If you've got a problem, come to the consulate during office hours," said the man angrily. Thompson shoved him in the chest, sending him flying back into the room. The man looked at him, unsure whether to be angry or frightened. Thompson walked over to him and kicked his legs out from under him and the man fell in a heap.

"My mate's been in jail a while now," he said, "and you've not been very supportive." The man spread his hands wide in a show of non-comprehension.

"The tanker captain," said Thompson with a sigh. The man appeared exasperated.

"He caused a spill," he said.

"He did not cause a spill," said Thompson. "And you're going to sort it. Make it plain the British Government's not happy. If he were some blonde girl backpacker caught deliberately smuggling drugs, you'd have him out by now so don't tell me you can't do anything."

"Yeah, well what will you do if I don't," said the consul. Thompson kicked him in the face.

"I'll chop your dick off," said Thompson. The man paled. "I don't like prissy gay public school boys who talk down to me and don't do their job especially when it's my taxes which pay their wages. And you and I both know what this country's like and how easy it will be for me to do what I like to you. If I find that you've called the police, I will pay to have someone do what I said. So make a bloody effort. Sort out a decent lawyer. Lean on the right government people and sort it out." The consul wiped the blood out of his eyes. He was shaking. "You're lucky that I think you could do something if you wanted to and am going to leave you alive," said Thompson, "because if my friend dies of cancer in that jail, or of anything else come to that, someone in the British Government or officialdom has gotta pay and it's a lot easier to make that person someone out of the way here rather than someone at home with Special Branch etc... protecting him."

"You're mad," said the consul.

"Probably am," said Thompson. "Just think what forty years of semi- confinement at sea will have done to my brain. You'd better hope I don't come back here and I definitely will if you don't get my mate out of jail." He turned at the door. "Enjoy your ladyboy," he said, "and get my mate out of jail or he'll be the last ladyboy you do enjoy."

Roxanne was confused at the airport. She'd only ever been abroad on package holidays during which reps operated on the basis that their customers should not be expected to think.

She carried with her the standard assumption that all foreigners spoke perfect English when they wanted to, and, if they said that they didn't understand her, then they were just being difficult.

A small man came up to her. "Miss?" he said.

"I suppose I am," she answered.

"I am here for you," he told her. He grabbed her bag.

"Be careful," she said. "It's expensive." It was a fake Louis Vuitton but where she came from even fake Louis Vuittons could still be thought of as expensive. The little man smiled and dragged it behind him on its spindly wheels at a furious pace.

They climbed into a mini-van which was painted a ghastly purple and had over-sized wing mirrors and set off.

"Where is Warren?" she asked him.

"Working," said the little man. "Survey."

She looked at the trash in the streets and the dumped wrecks at the side of the road.

"Reminds me of home on a Friday night," she said. The little man nodded.

"The municipal council is very poor," he said.

"How is Warren?" she asked him.

"He very happy," said the little man. "He not party every night, only sometimes. Other guy go with girl every day. He not. He love you very much." He took his eyes off the road to turn and look at her reassuringly and startled her by flashing a gold molar in his wide smile. She turned away and went quiet and looked deep in thought.

"You say he not go with girl every day," she said.

"Definitely not," said the little man.

"But," she said and then they hit a terrific bump in the road and she bit her tongue when the force flung her jaw shut. She thought better about pursuing this line of conversation.

They started to pass some industrial and shipyard constructions and then pulled up onto the town strip. She looked at the drab concrete structure at the side of the van. "Your hotel," said the little man. He noticed her reluctance to get out. "Three star," he said encouragingly.

She climbed out and he handed her the handle of her suitcase and went in and spoke to the desk. He handed her the key. "This hotel have lift," he said proudly, pointing to an ancient looking contraption.

"I think I'd rather take the stairs," she said.

"Fifth floor," he told her. "Lift better." He looked about to go.

"Just a minute," she said. "When will Warren come?"

"He come latter. Don't worry, he probably come see you first, then go Maggie's. You meet Maggie. She special friend of seamen. Oh just a minute." He went to the counter and came back with a controller for the television and handed it to her.

In the room, she lay down on the bed, her disappointment bringing her down. She flicked the T.V. on and found that there were two channels on the hotel system, one showing a local film without dubbing, and the other a porn film which was in English. The phone rang and she looked around and found the receiver at her side and picked it up. It was the little man.

"I forgot to say," he said. "Don't go out on your own."

"Roxanne was a woman in a song me mam liked," said Roxanne. "It's about a man who is in love with a beautiful girl and doesn't want her to leave him." Maggie smiled indulgently. She turned to Warren.

"What a wonderful child," she said, "and so charmingly naive." Warren shifted uncomfortably. "If you were only to work for me my dear," she said, turning again to Roxanne.

"I'm a good girl," said Roxanne with embarrassment.

"All my girls are good," said Maggie. She flicked her eyes at Warren, inviting him to confirm this. He declined to comment.

Later on, Roxanne tried to have something out with Warren. "Warren," she said, "the taxi driver said..."

"The agent," said Warren.

"What?" she said, confused.

"He was the agent," said Warren. "He's not a taxi driver. He would be very upset to know that you thought that." Roxanne was flabbergasted. She was being put on the defensive, but she had a strong idea that she was the offended one here. She shook her head in frustration.

"Whatever," she said. "He told me that you don't go with girls every night."

"So what are you complaining about?" said Warren, and then before she could answer, he'd turned to the chief engineer and reminded him that it was his round.

"I buy my own," said the chief engineer grumpily.

"Tight Scottish git," said Warren quietly enough that the chief could hear it but not so loudly that he couldn't pretend that he hadn't.

The sergeant turned his head to follow the very young girl walking down the street. She was a teenager but walked like an adult with a precocious confidence. He smiled and tailed her.

In the apartment, he looked sternly at the mother and told her to get out. The mother, intimidated by his uniform, hurried out the door.

The girl looked at him defiantly, and he sat down in a kitchen chair and smiled at her.

"I'm sending you to jail," he said. "You will bring shame to me. I don't want underage girls working around here. The authorities don't like that and one of those foreign organisations might take an interest.

"I am still at school," she said. He nodded. "I will be ruined," she said. "I will never get a job." He nodded again.

"That's true," he said.

"I'm only doing it to feed my family," she said.

"That's what every criminal says," he told her.

"I'm not a criminal," she said.

"No you're not," he told her, "but I will still throw you in jail." She looked at his crotch. "Don't even think about it," he said.

"Then what do you want?" she asked him. He studied her carefully. She was quite sexy and with some care would prove irresistible.

"I threw your sister in jail you know," he said.

"Of course I know," she replied.

"I didn't throw her in jail because she was a prostitute," he told her, "I threw her in jail because she thought she could do what she liked without getting permission. You are turning out to be just the same." She just continued to stare at him. "If you do what I want and then tell anyone, you will disappear," he said.

"I am a big girl," she told him.

"You know Maggie?" he asked her.

"Of course" she said. She seemed too calm. He didn't like that, but, then again, maybe it was good for his purposes.

"She will sort you out," he said.

"I don't like it," said Maggie. "I don't want to be involved."

"You won't be involved, you just need to know what's going on so that you can sort it out a little bit. You know, make sure he follows the script." Maggie made a face.

"The authorities," she said.

"I am the authorities," he replied. She snorted.

"The real authorities," she said. He lost his temper.

"Listen," he told her, "I can shut you down anytime I like. You don't think I can? You want to try to take me on?"

"Calm down," she said.

"I'll calm down when you say you will do what I want," said the sergeant.

"I will do what you want," she said. The sergeant continued to stare at her for a moment and then turned and left.

The door stuck open and the sun threw an oblong of dust-ridden light into the dim interior and Maggie's pet boy appeared in it and looked at her thoughtfully.

"I don't like it," she said. She looked up at him. "I was a famous ballerina in China," she said.

"I know," he told her, and he stroked her hair.

The radio officer was with Warren and his girlfriend. He was describing his exploits with the prostitute and darting looks at Warren's girlfriend to see if she showed any sign of disapproval, at which he would instantly be filled with, what he considered to be entirely justified, hatred of her. It was a strange thing about merchant seamen. They took great pride in treating the most rancid thieving mercenary prostitute like a princess but hated all ship's wives and girlfriends not their own, though sometimes their own as well. There was a kind of sense that at least the prostitutes were openly trading sex for security whereas the wives were doing so more subtly and wouldn't admit it and were therefore hypocrites.

Warren's girlfriend didn't take the bait but just laughed which confused the radio officer. He wasn't sure that she fully understood and wondered whether he should go through the whole story again but decided not to.

"Be careful," said Warren. The radio officer scoffed.

"What are they going to do to me," he sneered. Warren was cowed.

Warren's girlfriend took him aside. "Warren, aren't we going to spend any time on our own?" she said. Warren seemed to be reluctant to comment on this idea. He liked to be part of the gang. He was already aware that they regarded him as soft because he'd brought her out. "I'm not embarrassing you am I?" she said. His eyes flicked up to her face to check if she meant it in a nasty way, but he looked into her own open eyes and realised that she meant it as an honest question. "I don't think that radio officer likes me," she said. "I'm not sure that any of them like me."

"They don't like anyone," said Warren in a rare moment of clarity.

"I shouldn't have come, should I," she said and he felt a twinge of guilt and shame. She looked at the floor. "I should go back to the hotel," she said.

She turned and went and Warren looked after her, mouth open, uncertain as to what he should do.

Suddenly Thompson was at his side. "Go after her," he said, "and don't come back until the morning."

"But I thought you thought...," said Warren.

"Never mind what you thought I thought," said Thompson. Warren stared at him and Thompson sighed. "Listen," he said, "if you're still in this bar in three seconds, I'll punch your lights out."

Thompson looked over to where the radio officer was still bragging about how he'd humiliated the sergeant in front of his own men. Idiot, thought Thompson. He knew that he, himself, would still get the blame if anything came of it even though he'd had no control over the situation.

The chief engineer and Thompson were in the engine control room. The chief looked sad. "I'm to blame," he said. "It's all over. I've ruined my son's life and I'm the cause of Roly's being in jail."

"How have you ruined your son's life?" said Thompson, confused.

"I've told Terry to sort him out with a job," said the chief.

"I still don't understand," said Thompson.

"I don't want him to follow me," said the chief. "He'll end up like us." Thompson didn't take offence. He just scoffed.

"By the time he gets through his tickets, it'll all be third world officers and he'll be a new build supervisor or a bastard manager like Terry," he said.

"And Roly?" said the chief.

"Well," said Thompson," you didn't cause the spill although you were supervising. Captains go to jail. The media's happy, the Government's happy. To be honest, I don't think Roly really cares that much. He hates his sons, he can't stand his wife, he never gets any time alone to enjoy his million pound house. He's all right in there. The company's crew sent word to look out for him."

"You're just saying that. I know you threatened the consul," said the chief. "You wouldn't have done that if you genuinely thought he was better off."

"Maybe I just didn't like the consul," said Thompson. "I hate superior gays talking down to me."

"That's not true," said the chief. "Whenever there has been one with this company, Terry put him with you, because he knew you would protect him. In any case, that doesn't make sense. You didn't know he was gay till you went round to his pad and saw the ladyboy."

"I knew he was superior," said Thompson.

"What will you do if he doesn't use his influence to get Thompson out?" said the chief intrigued.

"If I genuinely think that he hasn't made an effort, I will cut his dick off," said Thompson. "If I can see that he tried really hard and failed, that's fair enough, I'll just give him a kicking because he didn't try hard enough until someone threatened him."

"You're a fair man," said the chief. Thompson wondered if he was being sarcastic. "I should have been more careful," said the chief.

"It's not your fault if the equipment fails because the company won't pay to maintain it properly," said Thompson.

"Whose then?" asked the chief. "Terry's?"

"The accountants, the board's, the chairman's, the banks who control the loans, the Government which lets the banks rule everything. Who knows. Ill-informed journalists have to be able to point the finger at someone and that someone is Roly."

"He'll die in there won't he?" said the chief.

"I think so," said Thompson.

"While all the thieves and criminals in the U.K. wear their old school ties and throw stolen widows' and orphans' funds at strippers."

"You're starting to sound like Bob Dylan," said Thompson with a smile.

"I was a fan, believe it or not," said the chief.

"Can you play Knocking' on Heaven's Door on the guitar?" asked Thompson.

"I can," said the chief.

The lady journalist sipped her iced tea and Thompson looked at her, carefully evaluating her. He didn't like British people who drank iced tea which he considered to be a vile American custom.

"It's a human interest story," she said. The cafe was full of cigarette smoke. She did not seem to be bothered by this which, he decided, was in her favour. Maybe she wasn't some right-on leftie. He decided to hold off on despising her until he found out more. "You say he's a highly competent captain," she said. Thompson nodded. "So why did the company abandon him?" she asked.

"Because they are bastards," said Thompson. He didn't smile. She didn't seem to be bothered by his abrupt reply. He was beginning to like her.

"Is he being treated well?" she asked. "I didn't feel he could really answer that himself honestly while the guards were there."

"He isn't complaining," said Thompson.

"Exactly what happened?" she said. Thompson sighed.

"Something was broken. To save the company money they just pumped something over the side."

"The company knew?" she asked him.

"Officially no, unofficially yes," he said.

"Is that normal," she asked.

"Of course," he said. "These days the captain is only on board to take the rap for breaking the rules which have to be broken to stay in business. Look at the ferries. Slow right down in fog every time to comply with the regulations, you'll soon be fired and the only people who go to prison for corporate crimes are whistleblowers, unless the security services get them first."

"You seem to have a bee in your bonnet about that," she said.

"I sailed with a radio officer who was ex-Royal Corps of Signals. He said he was ex-SAS. They always have a signalman in their platoons apparently, and he implied that they used to bump people off for just finding out things. That's why I think it's a joke that all these political paedophiles get off scot-free and Roly goes to jail because he killed a few seagulls, maybe. Hypocritical bastards."

"Hmm," she said. "The paedophile thing is not relevant unless your friend is also in jail for that." She flicked her eyes up from her notepad. "The fact that the politicians are all hypocrites protecting the business is. You don't need to keep saying bastard. I can't quote that. I understand the frustration."

"You could help him but you won't," said Thompson. "No editor is going to see any profit in defending someone who killed innocent little animals." He thought for a moment. "Even if half the readers like angling as a hobby?" He laughed. "Everyone's a hypocrite." He looked at her steadily. "Would you really like to get him out? I thought journalists were only interested in ethnic minority dissidents getting out of jail, not ordinary people."

"My father humbled me," she said. "I was doing a story on exactly such a dissident and he told me about this appalling story. He is an ex-merchant navy captain."

"Maybe I know him?" he said.

"Do you know anyone with my surname?" she asked him.

"No I don't," said Thompson. "You're not married then?"

"Career girl," she said, "and my child-bearing years are nearly over."

"That's only a problem if you wanted them," he said.

"I didn't. I do now," she answered. He wondered what to say. I'm sorry didn't seem appropriate but what did. "Malnutrition usually gets people like your friend when they're in third world jails," she said. "The consul is supposed to take him food or have someone do it."

"The consul is too busy with his ladyboy," said Thompson. He reminded himself to be careful not to seem too bitter. If he had to do something to the consul, he didn't want the finger to be pointed at him too soon, not until he'd left the country either on this ship, or on a plane to join another one. "You didn't meet the consul did you," said Thompson.

"No," she said, "perhaps I should have taken the opportunity."

"What do you really think will happen?" he said.

"I think your friend will stay in jail for a few years. His health will suffer. The Government will fully abandon him if it hasn't already. Eventually, some new trade deal will be up for grabs and the government here will throw your friend's early release into the deal as a gesture of goodwill. The British Government could make the foreign aid which they hand over every year dependent upon your friend's release but they won't, because they will consider in their warped way that that could be viewed as improper, whereas leaving your friend to rot in jail is just letting things take their natural course."

"Do you know that when the Royal Navy fired a salute in imperial China and accidentally killed someone, the captain just handed over a random seaman to be strung up."

"They are no better than you are. Yes, I've heard it all before from my father," she said.

"I meant the British Government whom that captain was representing were immoral," said Thompson. She shrugged. "I've never met anyone as cynical as I am," he told her. She shrugged again.

"I've been around," she said. Thompson decided he did like her.

"How'd you like to get drunk in here with me and then go up to your room and have sex?" he asked her.

"I still might abandon this story and your friend," she said.

"It's all over for Roly anyway," said Thompson.

Warren was knocking gently on the lady journalist's door. Thompson swung the door open and stood looking at him, annoyed and curious at the same time. Warren would never have come looking for him unless it was quite an emergency.

"The agent came to the ship," he said.

"And?" said Thompson.

"Roly's been stabbed," said Warren. Thompson swore.

"What is it?" said the lady journalist.

"Roly's been stabbed," said Thompson.

"Is he alive?" she asked. Thompson looked thoughtful. He had just assumed he was.

"Is he?" he asked Warren.

"At the moment," said Warren.

"O.K," said Thompson, "I'm coming to the ship. I want to see the bosun. Telephone the agent and tell him to book me a ticket down there for this afternoon."

"I want to come too," said the lady journalist.

"Tell him to book one on the company account and another one for which someone else will pay," he said. "Just a minute," he continued. "I'll pay for the other one. You got your passport?" he said to the woman.

"Will a copy do?" she asked him.

"Yeah," said Thompson. She climbed out from under the bed sheets and, stark naked, walked across to her handbag and pulled out a copy of her passport and walked over to them and handed it to Warren. Warren was quite surprised. He had never seen such a fine looking woman over forty naked. He took the paper and disappeared. Thompson turned to look at her. She shrugged and went over to the bathroom. "Gave him a thrill, I suppose," said Thompson.

Thompson confronted the bosun. "You told me you were looking after him," said the captain. The bosun pleaded for understanding.

"There are many gangs," he said. "We bribe one, another gang attack him."

"Bribery," said Thompson. "You mean you were paying? I thought they were doing it because he had been good to your nationality's crew." The bosun threw his arms wide in supplication.

"Captain, they are criminals in there. They don't do anything for nothing." Now the bosun was making Thompson feel as if he were a naive kid.

"How much did you pay total?" he asked.

"Five hundred dollars," said the bosun.

"I'll give you that," said Thompson. The bosun shook his head.

"We don't want it," he said. "We are ashamed."

"All right," said Thompson. "All right. I'll go down there and see if I can sort this mess out. I hope that the prison authorities take better care of him now."

"Maybe the British Government will help now," said the bosun. Thompson snorted.

"No chance," he said. "He killed seabirds. That's worse in the British media than carpet bombing some inoffensive nation."

The plane down was a propellor plane and Thompson could see that the journalist was enjoying it. "I suppose you'll write about this now," he said.

"Oh, I'll write it but I can't make them print it," she said. In any case, if there are any arms deals going and the Government doesn't want any publicity about this, they just won't be able to print it anyway. Free press is a relative term."

The prison hospital was marginally better than the main prison. Roly had a tube up his nose and looked very pale. Thompson had a desire to stroke his forehead but was afraid such a gesture would appear homosexual. "I've known him more than thirty years," he said. The journalist didn't comment. Thompson looked at the blood soaked bandage around his waist. "Don't change the bandages too frequently do they," he said. "Shame he's not conscious. I'd at least like him to know we've been here."

The doctor, having suffered Thompson's implied criticism of his care silently, generously offered the advice that he would be awake if they came back later. "There are no visiting hours for hospital patients," he said. "You can come anytime."

"That's quite kind of the authorities," said the journalist.

"It's because the patients might die anytime and the families might miss a last chance to see them otherwise," said the doctor.

"We're overwhelmed by your charity," said Thompson. The doctor smiled pleasantly.

They hung around in a stuffy cafeteria and went back later. Roly groaned with pain and said "'Hi," through clenched teeth.

"What did you do Roly?" said Thompson smiling. "Turn someone down for sexual favours?"

"Offended someone," Roly replied. "Have you told my wife, not that she'd care."

"Terry probably will," said Thompson.

"Her first question will be, how long has he got to live," said Roly.

"Come on," said Thompson, "she's not that bad."

"I'm insured for half a million," said Roly.

"Well," Thompson admitted, "that might make a difference."

"Maybe they'll get me out now," said Roly. Thompson shot a glance at the journalist.

"We're working on it," he said. "The bosun is sorry."

"He shouldn't be," said Roly. "His influence kept me safe and sound for a good few months. He certainly did more for me than the British Government."

"You killed seabirds Roly," said Thompson, "deliberately."

"I never thought about them," said Roly. "Mind you, I bet that's a line the Nazis used at Nuremberg."

"You're hardly a Nazi war criminal," said Thompson.

"I'm being treated the same if not worse," said Roly wallowing in self-pity.

"Come on, perk up. You're alive. Sooner or later you'll get out," said Thompson. You'll never get another job at sea again, so you can just sit in your garden like you've always wanted to do and nothing your wife says will make any difference. If she gets on your nerves, you can just get a job stacking shelves or go down the pub." Roly laughed and then winced and clutched at his stomach.

"Don't do that," said the journalist. He shouldn't do that should he," she said, turning to the doctor. The doctor shrugged and continued to smile.

The radio officer sat in Maggie's and smiled at the underage girl who shifted her skirt, displaying her fantastic legs to their best advantage. Maggie leant down and whispered in his ear. "That is my auntie's daughter," she said, "in from the countryside. She is not available. She is a nice girl;

she is too young." She saw the scorn on the radio officer's face. Stupid man, she thought. So easy to manipulate. Can't even see a set-up like this. She imagined the judge adding years to the sentence when the prosecuting attorney asked her, "And did you inform the defendant that the victim was underage?" and she answered in the affirmative.

The radio officer slid a hand over the girl's thigh and she fluttered her eyelashes at him. Some of the other officers were looking at him and either registered alarm or envy. Maggie's pet boy turned to her and raised his eyebrows, a sign of resignation.

"I don't like it," said Maggie.

"You don't have any choice," said her pet boy. "The sergeant will shut you down."

Over the other side of the room, Roxanne was beginning to feel frustration. "Warren, I came to be with you," she said.

"Well, we're together aren't we," he replied.

"Yes, but you're not the same when you're with them," she said. Warren looked at the floor. "Please Warren," she said, tugging at his arm. "Let's go somewhere where we can be alone." Warren felt the stubbornness kicking in, but somehow, there was just a sliver of rationality fighting with it, and he realised that if he didn't go with her out of this bar right now, he was lost. He was on the road to a Thompson-like existence.

"I'm worried about him," he said, looking towards the radio officer. Her eyes followed his.

"Warren, he's ten years older than you," she said. "He can look after himself." She thought that girl does look young, but she could feel that she was pulling ahead and didn't want any distractions.

Warren left with her.

The chief engineer was in another bar. "Hello Dad," said a voice behind him. He turned to look at the speaker and his jaw fell open. "Happy birthday," said the boy who was standing there. "The agent told me you were in this bar."

"What are you doing here?" said the chief. He liked this bar because it didn't play music and if he strained he could just about hear what people were saying.

"Other people from school and university were taking a year off to go round the world, I thought I could take a little while off and go and see my Dad. Mum was all right with it."

"You haven't come to blame me for something?" said the chief engineer. The boy looked puzzled.

"Why would I blame you for something? What did you ever do to me?" he said.

"I dinnae know," said the chief. He indicated the empty stool at his side. "Sit yourself down," he said. The boy sat down. "You're not in any trouble?" he asked him.

"No," said the boy. "What makes you think I might be?" The engineer shrugged.

"When I was home a few times ago, you were in trouble for fighting at school." The boy laughed.

"One fight Dad."

The chief engineer was smiling. It was such a rare event that the muscles in his face genuinely hurt.

"And you don't hate me?" The boy looked confused.

"Why do you keep saying that?" he asked.

"I just assumed you did," said the chief.

"What did I ever do to make you think that?" asked the boy. The chief engineer smiled more broadly.

"It's my birthday," he said.

"I know," said the boy. He put his arm around his father.

The radio officer woke up in the sagging bed in the seedy hotel and watched the young girl getting dressed with a satisfied smile on his face. Her slim figure made him want her again. He tried to engage her in conversation but she seemed embarrassed for some reason which he did not understand.

"Goodbye," she said, slinging her handbag over her shoulder. The radio officer shrugged and leaned over to the side table and lit a cigarette and watched her walk out.

Suddenly the door burst open and the sergeant and one of his men walked in. "A complaint has been received," he said. "From a thirteen-year-old girl." The radio officer's jaw hung open.

"No way is she thirteen," he said.

"She is thirteen," said the sergeant. "We take this sort of thing very seriously."

"I didn't know," said the radio officer.

"You were warned," said the sergeant.

"That's not true," said the radio officer. He suddenly realised how the sergeant was here so quickly. He sighed.

"O.K, I'll pay," he said, slumping.

"Attempting to bribe a policeman is a very serious offence," said the sergeant.

"You're joking right," said the radio officer.

"We are taking you into custody," said the sergeant. He adopted a very serious tone. "You will no doubt be anxious that the British consul be informed. I will of course see to that but I believe you will find that they are not always keen to offer their utmost assistance to paedophiles."

"I'm not a paedophile," said the radio officer. The sergeant laughed.

"By the time this gets to court, we will have her in her school uniform without any make up and she will look about ten," he said. "Repeat that if you like. I will just deny it. You won't even be able to understand what is said in court anyway. And your lawyer will be a joke."

When the constable had handcuffed him, the sergeant spoke again. "Don't worry too much," he said. "You'll be out in five, or maybe ten, years."

The agent told Thompson and watched him slump into a heap. "I told him," he said. "I told him. O.K, what will it take to get him out?"

"This is a little difficult," said the agent. "I believe that the sergeant truly wants to see him go to jail."

"That will not be good for him," said Thompson. "It will let his bosses know that he allows underage prostitution in his town."

"Such is the sergeant's hatred for your radio officer, he is prepared to put up with that," said the agent.

Thompson sighed. "First Roly and now him. What happened to the days of the British Empire when we could do what we liked and no one could touch us."

"Mr Churchill is no longer your Prime Minister and in any case we were never in the British Empire," said the agent a little testily. He thought for a moment. "The sergeant might come round. It depends how much he wants to humiliate your man. He'll definitely have flung him into the communal cell for a while. That will not be pleasant."

"I suppose I should go to see him," said Thompson. "Maggie was in on this?" he said.

"I don't know. I should think so. The sergeant won't have given her any choice," replied the agent.

Thompson spoke to the radio officer through the bars. "Why did you do it, you idiot?" he said.

"She didn't look thirteen," pleaded the radio officer.

Oh, so she only looked fifteen," said Thompson. The radio officer gnawed at his lip. "Captain, help me," he said.

"Why didn't you just pay the sergeant off last time," said Thompson bitterly. "You've caused everyone problems now. The company will just delight in blaming me for this. "Captain, you did not exercise proper authority over your crew," he quoted from a past incident, "or some such rubbish. The eighteen year olds look fifteen anyway. Isn't that enough. Why did you think you had to have to get a fifteen year old who looked thirteen."

"She didn't look thirteen," said the radio officer plaintively.

Thompson continued. "And you let them contact the British consul. That's made it official now. Now you put me at risk if I try and bribe your way out of this and it makes it harder for the sergeant to suddenly reverse everything." Thompson thought about this. "He really must not care about the money anymore," he said. Thompson looked at the other criminals through the bars. "The natives are not looking friendly," he said.

The radio officer turned to look at their stony expressions. "I don't think you need to worry yet," said Thompson. "They know not to touch you without the sergeant's permission and, in a while, you'll probably be taken off his hands and he won't want you beaten-up or worse when he hands over custody." He turned to go. "Just remember," he said. "You're guilty. You did it."

"But I didn't know," said the radio officer.

"Yeah, yeah,

"Roly is guilty. He did it," said the radio officer.

"Don't compare yourself to Roly," said Thompson. "The company leaned on him and an oil spill is not the same, it doesn't matter what the lefties say. And if people like him didn't take chances the world would stop turning." He realised he was off on his usual rant, and what's more, didn't think the radio officer worthy of listening to it. He left him.

The sergeant appeared before his victim and smiled at him through the bars, his gold tooth adding to his vicious image as he had known it would when he had it fitted. The radio officer looked at him until he went away.

The lady journalist sat up in bed, her breasts showing over the top of the sheet, and looked at

Thompson where he was pulling off his shirt. "This changes everything you know," she said.

"What do you mean?" he asked her.

"I can't do anything for your friend while another of your crew is up for paedophilia," she said. Thompson sighed.

"It's not paedophilia," he said. "She was thirteen."

"If it were at home, they would be slinging the book at him," she said. "You're old enough to know how things work. My editor is not going to be interested. It's a stretch to defend your friend but at least there's an angle in building up the big corporate villain behind the scenes but then what happens, it transpires that another one of you is up for paedophilia and your friend will be forgotten anyway and all I will have achieved is that I embarrassed my newspaper and turned myself into a pariah, probably an unemployed one."

"Well, no one asked you to help anyway," said Thompson.

"Don't be like that," she said. "You know I wanted to. This idiot ruined it for you. You should leave him to rot."

"I might have to," said Thompson.

"You're sure it isn't just about money," she said. "Look where we are. Money is all that matters around here."

"Same everywhere," said Thompson, "but we're dealing with loss of face."

"You care about them both don't you," she said, "your friend and this idiot."

"It's my job," said Thompson. He sat down beside her on the bed. "I'm like a father," he said.

Then he looked at the floor. "I'm getting too old for this game," he continued. "Too old and too tired. And I'm sick of being on the defensive all the time."

"Should have become a funeral director," she said, "the world always needs them and there's not much you can do wrong. You can't really make a corpse any the worse. It's still a corpse."

"An accountant," said Thompson. "That's the only profession the Government values."

"Lawyer," she said.

"I have some principles," said Thompson.

"So what are you going to do?" she said trying to bring the conversation back from its philosophical course.

"Not much I can do," said Thompson. "If the Government doesn't care, the company doesn't care, their families don't care. Actually," he said, "that's not entirely fair, "the radio officer's family wants to help him, Roly's wife doesn't care if he dies."

"Is she really like that?" asked the journalist.

"Aren't all women?" asked Thompson.

"Not all women," she said. "Only wharf-side hookers and women you marry and then desert and are unfaithful to every time your company sends you onto a ship."

"You know something," said Thompson., "I never was unfaithful to my wife, not once. At least not until she threw me out after our daughter died."

"How did she die?" asked the journalist.

"Suicide," said Thompson. "I think my wife had enough of me moping and could see that I blamed her and myself."

"You probably were to blame," said the journalist.

"We were," said Thompson.

"How did she do it?" asked the journalist.

"On the tube," said Thompson. "Held up the trains." She didn't know whether he was joking or not.

"I want to help your friend," she said. "Believe me. I can't point to a single thing I've actually achieved as a journalist. I helped raise a bit of pointless hysteria on occasion, but I don't think that's really an achievement. If I were to get your friend out..."

"Even though he's guilty," said Thompson.

"Even though he's guilty," she said.

The young girl's mother was distraught. "What are you involved in?" she asked. "I told you to stay away from the police. Oh, you will go to jail too, just like your sister."

"Mother," she said. "It is in the hands of the sergeant."

"You will have to give evidence," said her mother.

"The sergeant will tell me what to say," said the girl.

"What is the sergeant paying you?" asked the mother with a sudden avaricious gleam in her eye.

"He is not throwing me in jail," said the girl. The mother bit her lip.

"Why were both my daughters so stupid?" she said.

"You will see mother," said the girl. "I will do good for the sergeant and one day I will be like Maggie with my own place and you will be happy with me then."

The chief's son stood beside him in the vast engine room. "Impressive eh?" said the chief. His son said something but the chief couldn't hear him and waved him into the control room. Inside this air-conditioned sanctuary, they sat down with cups of tea.

"I dinnae think you should follow me," said the chief.

"What made you think I wanted to?" said his son.

"Your mother said something," replied the chief. The boy laughed.

"It was just a passing thought, more of a joke really."

"Your life will pass you by," said the chief.

"I won't do it," said the boy. "I thought of doing something creative anyway. I don't know, maybe advertising, something like that. Of course, I'd have to go to university."

The chief engineer doubted his hearing. He wanted to say, I have been so worried but thought it might appear pathetically weak but then he decided that time with his son was limited and there should be only honesty between them.

"I have been so worried," he said. His son patted him on the back.

"No need," he said. The chief had not been patted on the back for over forty years. He was a little discomfited.

"You don't bear any grudge against me?" he asked. The boy seemed mystified.

"Why?" he asked.

The chief was on the point of saying, your mother always gave me the impression that you did but then thought why cause a complicated little problem.

"I admire you," said the boy. "You sailed round the world. I never will."

"I dinnae do much," said the chief. "I just kept the engine going."

"More than a lot of people could?" said the boy.

"And how about girlfriends?" asked the chief. The boy shrugged.

"I've got one but I don't think I will be getting married young. I bet that's what you're worried about.

"Boy, you are smart," said the chief.

"You are too, you were just where no one was ever going to notice it," said the boy.

"How long will you stay?" said the chief.

"You know I can't stay forever," said the boy.

"How long?" said the chief. The boy was alarmed by the stress and the element of pleading in his father's voice.

"I don't know. A while." he said. "I'm in no hurry really."

"What do you think of the town?" said the chief, relieved and deciding to try and lighten the atmosphere.

"It's like home except at home you don't have to pay for it," said his son cheerfully.

"Boy, you are smart," said the chief.

When the chief's son went up to the officers' bar, the third mate's girlfriend was the only one in there.

"Hi," he said. She held out her hand formally.

"I'm Warren's girlfriend," she said. The boy looked confused. "Warren, the third mate," she said as if she were speaking to a retard.

"I'm not crew," said the boy. "I don't know all the officers."

"Really?" she said.

"Yeah, I'm the chief's son," he said. "I just came in for a coke."

"Oh," she said. "I thought you looked a bit clean and eh..."

"And what?" he asked.

"Normal," she said.

"They aren't normal?" asked the boy.

"Well, you know," she said.

"I don't think they'd like to hear you talking about them like that," said the boy.

"Will you tell them then?" she asked him.

"No," he said.

"Have you seen Warren?" she asked him.

"I don't know who he is," said the boy patiently. She flushed.

"Yes, of course," she said. She amused him.

"Where are you from?" he asked her.

"South Shields," she told him. He looked confused. "It's on the Tyne," she said. "And you?"

"Down South," he said.

"Well, I could tell that," she snorted.

"Some little commuter town," he said.

"But your Dad is Scottish," she said.

"He met my mother when he was injured in Southampton and she was working in the hospital and then they bought a house where she was from. That's why I don't wield a Stanley knife and am not an alcoholic," he said.

"You can't say that," she gasped.

"I'm only joking," he said.

"You can't joke like that," she told him. "And it isn't funny. Don't joke like that in front of these sailors. They are very dangerous and they take offence very easily."

"O.K., I won't," he said.

"You're not at university here," she said.

"O.K., O.K.," he said. "Anyway, I'm not at university at home yet. I just left school, but I might go back and do some more and then go to university."

"I thought chief engineers' sons became captains and captains' sons became chief engineers'," she said.

"My dad doesn't want me to go to sea," he told her.

"You shouldn't," she said. "You don't want to be like them."

"Your boyfriend is one of them?" said the boy. She nodded.

"My fiancé sort of, technically," she said.

The bar suddenly filled up with the officers coming in for their smoko. Warren glanced at the boy. "This is the chief engineer's son," said Roxanne. Warren nodded and the chief engineer's son shifted slightly. Warren wasn't intimidating but he'd still been having an intimate conversation with his girlfriend, or fiancée, or whatever she was.

The lady journalist was fuming. The sergeant would not allow her in for the interview and, what was worse was she was sure he wasn't making her stay outside because she was a journalist, but because she was a woman. He had actually laughed when she said she was a journalist for a London paper. "Not possible," he had said. She had shot a look at Thompson to see if he reacted. There may have been a flicker of a smile. She couldn't be sure, but, then again, what could she expect from him. If she wanted to be with some neutered new man, there were plenty around.

The consul and the lawyer and the agent and Thompson sat on one side with the radio officer, and the prosecutor and the sergeant sat on the other. There were no security guards. Everyone, apart from possibly the consul on diplomatic grounds, would have been shot dead long before they made it out of the main entrance if there were an escape attempt, and where would they go anyway.

"The fact of the matter is you're guilty," said the prosecutor. The radio officer reddened.

"This is a vicious persecution because I didn't pay a bribe last time," he said. Thompson raised his eyes to the ceiling. The man was a complete fool.

"So, this is not the first time that you have done this?" said the prosecutor.

"I mean the first time the sergeant asked me for a bribe," said the radio officer. The lawyer turned white.

"Has the sergeant asked you for a bribe to see you released from these current charges?" asked the prosecutor.

"No, but..." began the radio officer. The prosecutor waved him to be silent.

"You admit the charges, you had sex with this very young girl," he said.

"They all look young," said the radio officer.

"Just shut up," burst out Thompson.

The consul was smiling an evil little smile. It was the same consul as Thompson had visited in the South. His colleague was on sudden sick leave and he was handling both consulates temporarily.

"Seems your crew just can't control themselves captain," he said.

"Whose side are you on?" said Thompson.

"There is no British Empire now and there is no law of extraterritoriality," said the prosecutor, "not that this was ever part of the British Empire and not that we would have allowed that law to stand." His family was ethnic Chinese and he bore a grudge.

"Listen," said Thompson. "I'm sure this can all be sorted out. Why don't we leave the agent and the sergeant to sort it out quietly?" The prosecutor smiled and slung the local paper across to him. The radio officer and the girl in question in her school uniform were on the front page. Thompson sighed. "It'll take months to come to trial won't it?" he said.

"Possibly years," said the prosecutor. "However; if the judge is feeling lenient, he might take time served into account when it comes to sentencing, which it inevitably will."

Thompson glared at the consul. "Why don't you say something?" he said. "What do we pay our taxes for?"

"What do you expect me to do?" said the consul. "It's an open and shut case. He did it. What do you think the foreign office is going to say if they find I've been battling away for a paedophile who is in any case guilty?" he asked.

Thompson reddened. "Will you kindly stop using that word?" he said.

The sergeant laughed. Thompson glared at him.

"Your client will be transferred to the local prison," said the prosecutor to the lawyer in their native language. Thompson looked at him quizzically.

"He transfer the prison," said the lawyer.

"Marvellous," said Thompson. "He gets a lawyer who can't even speak English fluently.

"He's free," said the prosecutor. "Your company declined to pay for a decent lawyer. Your agent told me." The agent twitched.

They left the room and the lady journalist said, "I heard everything, they might as well have let me in."

"The sergeant just wanted to humiliate a white woman," said Thompson.

"Can't you just pay?" she said.

"You heard them," replied Thompson. "It's front page news now."

"Yes, in this dead and alive hole," she responded. Thompson shrugged.

"It means a bigger operation to bury it now. These guys might want tens of thousands. The company won't pay bribes on principle, not for him anyway. They'd pay a bribe in ten seconds flat to get a ship out of the country."

"Stop being so cynical and start being constructive," she said. "I can't help your friend until you do something about this idiot."

"I wish I could just shoot him," said Thompson with a sigh. She looked at him steadily. "That was a joke." he said.

"Life is cheap here," she answered.

"You sure you don't just want to get a big story out of springing Roly? Are you sure that's not your motive?" Thompson asked.

"What do you think? she said.

"I don't know," he answered.

"Of course it is," she told him.

The chairman and Terry sat in their offices looking out over the Thames.

"Idiots," said the chairman.

"Boys will be boys," said Terry.

"You're the manager, I expect you to recruit suitable people," said the chairman. Terry scoffed.

"I got you suitable people, a nice weak captain like Roly who let us bamboozle him into not worrying about the broken separator," he replied. The chairman didn't like that.

"And that other idiot?" he said.

"That's just human frailty," said Terry. "You want to avoid that, don't employ humans."

"What should we do?" asked the chairman

"It's best not to defend Roly. We don't want any publicity. We forced him to do it, but we need deniability as our American friends say," replied Terry.

"So leave him to rot," said the chairman. "Even though he's been stabbed." Terry shrugged. "Suit us if he died really wouldn't it," the chairman continued.

"Yeah," said Terry. Terry had once swindled a Filipino widow out of her compensation by using the fact that her husband hadn't been wearing safety boots when a steel wire snapped and decapitated him and therefore hadn't been following correct safety procedures. The widow didn't have any money to sue, because Terry had swindled her out of it, and the Government let things like this go.

"How long have you known Roly?" asked the chairman.

"Twenty years," said Terry.

"And you don't care about him?" said the chairman.

"Nah," said Terry.

"You are a bastard," said the chairman. Terry scoffed again.

"Don't give me that," he said. "You'd slit your own grandmother's throat to make the company an extra cent."

"All right, all right," said the chairman. "What about the other one? It's better for us if he's found innocent. Maybe we should get him a decent lawyer."

"There won't be any publicity," said Terry. "Who cares about him. Anyway, it's better for us. Any sobbing, bleeding heart, journalist who wants to take up Roly's case will soon lose interest if he finds out one of his crew was found guilty of paedophilia,"

"He was guilty of the offence after Roly had been replaced by Thompson," said the chairman.

"Who cares?" said Terry. "Fine distinctions don't bother journalists."

"I thought Thompson was a ...," said the chairman.

"A stand up guy," said Terry. The chairman frowned.

"You picked up too many americanisms on your little sojourn," he said. Terry looked at him.

"Thompson's tired and he doesn't care anymore," he said. "He might even be sympathetic to him, he's been a lot more tolerant of human frailty since his daughter died."

"Committed suicide," said the chairman. He was silent for a while. "So we do nothing," he said.

"In the words of Willie Whitelaw, sometimes when you absolutely must do something, the best thing is to do nothing," said Terry.

The chief engineer's son and Roxanne were sitting in the breakfast room of the hotel in which they were both staying. The chief engineer's son thought that she looked nice. Her features were a bit plain, but it all added to the attraction of her unsophisticated air.

"So you will get married?" he said.

"Oh, I don't know," she told him. "He's never asked me." The chief engineer's son wanted to say do you love him, but he knew that that would be a far too intimate question. "Do you think that he goes with those women?" she asked him. She was staring at him intently, and he felt uncomfortable. He wanted to say yes, but he didn't want to mess with a merchant seaman. He knew from his father's friends who occasionally came round the house that they were unpredictable when it came to violence. And I don't know would not be a satisfactory answer if it were to be found out he had given it.

"No," he said, "I don't."

"Would you?" she said smiling.

"I don't think so," he said.

"Don't think so?" she repeated. "So you think you might if you'd been at sea for months." The chief engineer's son squirmed. Again, if he answered in the affirmative he could be construed as saying that he thought Warren might. He shrugged.

"That's what I'm frightened off," she said sadly.

"Well, if you weren't to know." said the chief engineer's son.

"Don't say that," she said. "Please." He reached out an arm and touched her on the shoulder.

"You're just imagining things," he said. He was beginning to see why his mother had always refused to visit his father on any of his ships. Ignorance is bliss.

Thompson stood on the balcony of the mama-san's place and looked thoughtful. "It weren't us," she said. He turned to look over the road, resting on his folded arms on the wrought iron railing.

"So?" he asked.

"So, you know," she said.

"Maggie?"

"You know," she said.

"That poor boy is going to really go through it," he told her. She shrugged.

"He knew," she said. "That is why no one has any sympathy."

"Things have certainly changed since the old days," he said.

"In your country too," she replied.

"Yes, everywhere," he answered. "I told you about my friend in the South."

"You said he is guilty too," she said. He sighed.

"Guilt is relevant isn't it," he suggested.

"You are with that journalist," she said accusingly. "The blondie."

"If it makes you feel any better," said Thompson, "she's not a real blonde."

"It doesn't make me feel any better," she said. She joined him in leaning over the balcony. "The sergeant will not give up. He wants to humiliate your boy."

"You know," he said, "when I was young, if the captain told you to leave something alone, you left it alone, but these young people are so filled with their own self-importance, they don't listen and now look."

"Sleep with me," she said. Thompson thought about saying, "I'm with someone now." He thought about the lady journalist's body. Then he thought, who am I kidding.

"O.K.," he said.

He sat down in Maggie's place and pleaded with her. "I need you to get her to drop her complaint," he said.

"Speak to her," said Maggie, a little embarrassed.

"Come on," said Thompson.

"I don't think you care about that boy," she said.

"Honestly, I don't, but I can't get my friend out of jail in the South if I don't get him out too. This woman won't help me if I don't get this thing here to disappear.

"Get your boy here to commit suicide," said Maggie. Thompson looked at her with a stunned expression. "Technically," said Maggie. They were both silent for a moment. "You don't care about him. He commits suicide, there is no conviction," she added.

"I'm not a killer," said Thompson.

"So you don't want to sort it out yourself, but you want me to do it," she said.

"It happened in your club," he said accusingly.

"So," she said.

"Please," he pleaded.

"The sergeant," she said again as if there were nothing more to be said.

"Should I see the sergeant?" he asked her.

"If you want to humiliate yourself," she told him.

"I have to try," he said.

"Your company," she told him. "Why don't they help?"

"Honestly," he said, "it's the money, but they will use this paedophilia thing as an excuse to abandon their employee. They will more or less plead their own virtue as a defence."

"See the sergeant if you want," she said, "but you will just humiliate yourself.

Thompson sat on the wooden chair in front of the sergeant's desk. "How much is this going to cost me?" he asked.

"Your company is very rich," said the sergeant.

"The company won't pay," said Thompson

"Ten thousand dollars," he told him.

"That's more than normal," said Thompson.

"This is not a normal situation," the sergeant told him. "Normally, defendants do not humiliate me in front of my men."

"The company won't pay," repeated Thompson. "I will have to pay. I can't afford ten thousand." The sergeant appeared to soften.

"All right, five thousand," he said.

"I could buy a car with that," said Thompson.

"I will buy a car with that," said the sergeant.

"I don't know if I can get it," said Thompson.

"You will," said the sergeant, "or your boy stays in jail."

The bank didn't listen to Thompson. "We can't just send money there like that," they said. "And you will lose interest, you know, if you take that money out of your savings account without thirty days' notice." Thompson felt like biting the receiver.

"Just send the money," he said.

"Mr Thompson..." she began.

"It's Captain Thompson," he told her firmly

"I beg your pardon?" she said.

"It's Captain Thompson," he told her even more firmly. He was surprised at himself. He'd never insisted on being called Captain in his life."

"We cannot just send money like that Captain Thompson," she said. He put the receiver down.

Terry was indignant. "You want me to loan you five thousand to get a paedophile out of jail," he said.

"He's not a paedophile," said Thompson. "And I can't get Roly out of jail if I can't get him out because this lady journalist won't help me"

"How is she going to help you?" said Terry.

"You know, say it wasn't his fault, expose the conditions in which he's being kept."

Terry couldn't believe his ears. "You want me to help shift the guilt from Roly onto the company by loaning you five thousand dollars to bribe a policeman to get a paedophile out of jail." Thompson thought about it for a moment.

"Yeah," he said.

"Your personal life has really got to you," said Terry. "I'm going to do you a favour out of respect for the man you were and forget that we ever had this conversation." He put the phone down.

Roly's wife sat in the solicitor's office and smiled pleasantly at him. There was just a little something in her face; however, that made him feel a little uncomfortable. "How can I help?" he said.

"Well, I want to know the procedure for sorting out my husband's will," she told him.

"Your husband wants to make a will or he has recently died?" said the solicitor quietly.

"Neither," she replied. "I'm expecting him to die soon."

"Ah, he is terminally ill," said the solicitor. She appeared to become a little bit frustrated.

"No," she said. "However; I do expect him to die soon. He is in prison."

"Which one," said the solicitor, now thoroughly confused.

"In Asia," she said. "He's a merchant seaman. The solicitor didn't follow. "He caused a spill and he's been thrown in prison and he's been stabbed and he's got some intestinal problems apparently. I don't expect him to live very long," she said. "I just want to be prepared. I want to know if there'll be any hold-ups." She noticed the solicitor's slack jaw. "I've got two sons," she said as if that would clear everything up. The solicitor recovered and raised his eyebrows.

"You don't need a will," he said. "You're his wife, the consul will sort out a death certificate. Listen, have you asked the Government for help?"

"They're not interested," she said, emphatically. "He's guilty."

"Even so," said the solicitor. It didn't seem to him that she was all that interested either.

"There might be a complication," she said. The solicitor waited for her to speak.

"And?" he said. He had decided that she didn't really warrant sympathy.

"The company might sue his estate to protect themselves."

"Just a tactic," said the solicitor.

"But would that hold things up?" she asked him. He felt a twinge of malice.

"It might," he said carefully. "Do you think his death is imminent?" She pondered this.

"A month or so," she said, "with the poor medical care and the diet. I don't really know. I just want to be prepared. He has been very seriously ill and very seriously injured in a fight with another prisoner." The solicitor just wished she'd leave his offices. He rose from his chair.

"Just call me when it happens," he said, holding out his hand and leaving no opening for her to continue sitting in his offices.

The radio officer's mother was embarrassing Thompson. She was so grief-stricken over the fate of her son and such an obviously saintly woman that he didn't know how to deal with her. His father hadn't come. She'd said that he wanted nothing more to do with their son, which she considered very unfair, as he hadn't even been found guilty yet and, anyway, was their son. Thompson suspected that the father knew more than the mother about their son's past behaviour.

"I will be able to see him won't I?" she asked him pathetically. "I've come so far."

"You certainly have," said Thompson. He was sure that the sergeant would facilitate it. It would bring more humiliation and pain upon the radio officer's shoulders.

"He was such a good boy," she said. Thompson snorted. He had known the radio officer for a few years and knew that he was far from that. Still, he obviously had been nice to his mother apart from putting her through the ringer right now. "My husband wouldn't pay for my ticket," she said. "I had to use my life savings." Thompson sighed. He just spent his own life being caught up in one tragedy after another. "Can we see him today?" she asked him.

"He's at the jail now," he replied. "It'll take a little time to organise. Maybe tomorrow. Anyway, you've had a long flight."

"I brought some things for him," she said.

"All he wants or needs is cigarettes, I can assure you," said Thompson.

"Can I get some?" she said eagerly.

"It's all right," said Thompson kindly. "I take him some."

"If only he hadn't joined this profession," she said sadly.

"If only we all hadn't," he replied.

The screen was more of a nuisance than an effective barrier. Thompson sat back in the hard seat and watched the radio officer's mother speaking into the intercom. The radio officer had seemed to age, not as dramatically as Roly's fifty-five to eighty in a few months, but some nevertheless.

He could hear her quiet tones just underneath the singsong babble coming from the other booths. "Why do sons do this to their mothers?" he asked himself. "Such a good boy." What a joke.

He heard sobbing and looked up. She was clutching the side of the booth. The radio officer did not look like his usual cocky self. I just spend my whole life dealing with tragedy thought Thompson.

"I don't have that much money," said the boy's mother when they were standing outside the jail, and she was shielding her eyes from the bright sunlight. "Here," take my sunglasses," said Thompson, handing them to her. She put them on without seeming to notice he'd even handed them to her.

"I'll keep trying," he said.

"I can't stay here more than a few months," she said.

"Don't stay here at all," he told her. "It won't do any good and you'll just spend what little money you do have. I'll sort it out." She looked at him as if doubting him."

"I'll sort it out," he said.

"You're such a kind man," she told him.

"Yeah well," he said. "I did a lot of bad things when I was younger and I'm trying to do some good ones before I die." Then he realised that his usual brutal speech wasn't right for this situation."

"Did he do it?" she asked quietly. "They say that he admitted it."

"She is younger than she looks," he told her. "He was lonely. She more or less exploited him."

"His father says he doesn't want to know him anymore," she said.

"Yeah well, let he who is without sin...," said Thompson.

"We're not a religious family," she replied. "That's what my husband always says even though I attend mass. You see? You see what it's like?" He shrugged.

"British atheist eh," said Thompson. "Well, first remove the plank from your own eye before you complain about the splinter in someone else's, as Jesus said. Listen, I'll have the agent change your ticket and you fly home in the morning. You've done more than a lot of mothers would have. In fact, you're a bit of a saint."

"He's a good boy," she said.

"Yeah well, modern times. Standards have changed. I don't know what the answer is." He put his hand to her grey hair and stroked it back. "Try not to worry. He hasn't been convicted yet."

Thompson stood in his girlfriend's place. "You knew about this?" he asked her. The mama-san shrugged."

"Didn't happen in my place," she told him.

"You knew though. You could have warned us."

"It was obvious," she said. "Why did you mess with the sergeant? Where do you think you are? Anyway, he wouldn't have listened."

"Well, you're right there," he admitted.

"Why don't you go and see Maggie again?" she told him. Thompson looked up. Her pet boy was watching carefully from the other room.

"You're supposed to look after sailors," he told her. "That's your job."

"And yours," she said. She stared at him intensely. "Why do you care so much about him?" Thompson did care about him, but he didn't want to admit it.

"My friend, the former captain of this ship, is in jail and there's a lady journalist here who could maybe help to get him out, but she won't do anything while this is going on because her editors won't do anything if there is paedophilia involved.

"She was thirteen," said the mama-san. "Some girls here have had their second child at that age."

"Yes, but they don't view it like that at home," said Thompson. "Anyway, is she fifteen or thirteen?"

"You are sleeping with that journalist," said the mama-san.

He stood in Maggie's dusty place. Maggie was not feeling cooperative. "I can't believe you set him up," said Thompson.

"The sergeant is a very bad man," said Maggie. "What do you want me to do, lose my business for him, your radio officer. You warned him. He didn't listen. He is stubborn. We shall see how his stubbornness serves him in jail." Thompson sighed.

"What I want to know is can you get her to withdraw her statement?" Maggie laughed.

"In order to do that she'd have to go to the police station and sit in front of the sergeant. He'd have her in jail so long she wouldn't be able to work when she got out. She would be an old lady." She laughed again. "Like me," she said, "And who would want her then." She looked up at him. "Don't get involved," she said. "Don't try to speak to her. It was his own fault."

"You know Roly?" he said.

"Last dry dock," she told him.

"You want Roly to die in jail," he asked her. "Because he will if I can't get this boy out.

"He will anyway," she said. "He's already been stabbed. The diet is terrible. He's old. Why do you care about him? Why do you care about all these people? You didn't used to be like that." She looked at him slyly. You can't bring your daughter back to life by saving all these people who don't deserve your efforts. Roly is an experienced captain. He knew what he was doing. So the company leaned on him. Time for him to have been a man and just gone onto the blacklist and put up with it. He would survive. You can't be a captain as long as he has been and not have money."

"He didn't want to let the company down," said Thompson. She snorted.

"And the company really cared about him," she said.

"We can't all be cynical," said Thompson. "The world still needs good men in it."

"The world still needs victims," she said. "He is a victim; the radio officer is; you're not. Just be grateful and don't go looking for trouble. If trouble is due to you, it will arrive don't worry. You don't need more than your own share." She looked over at her pet boy. Thompson knew that the pet boy, effeminate as he seemed, would be an expert at one or another of the martial arts. "I don't want you coming here anymore," she said. "You and your crew are a problem and I don't need problems. Go to your girlfriend's. I wanted you. You slept with her just because she has a nicer ass.

Or go with that lady journalist. Strikes me, you are doing great." Thompson gave up and turned to the door. "Thompson," she said just as he was about to leave. "You're a good man. Be nice to yourself." Thompson paused in the doorway. "Go on, go," she said.

The chief engineer's son and Roxanne sat in bed. Roxanne's face was panic-stricken. "What have I done?" she said. The chief engineer's son said nothing. "I love Warren," she said. Could have fooled me, thought the chief engineer's son.

"No harm done," he said. "He need never know. You were lonely. I was around."

"You don't understand," she said. "I've been unfaithful to him."

"He's a merchant seaman," said the chief engineer's son.

"What does that mean?" she asked.

"Nothing," he said.

"It can't mean nothing," she replied. "You think he goes with those women don't you."

"I have no idea," he said. "They don't all. My father doesn't."

"You think," she said. "And I can't go back to him after you. He's like, he's like..."

"Like what?" said the chief engineer's son.

"Like a boy," she said. "You're so passionate. The chief engineer's son squirmed. This was far too intimate for him.

"Listen," he said. "I don't know why you Northern girls don't go down to the City of London, sit in some bar at lunchtime and wait for a commodities trader or something to pick you up. It'd take about five minutes. You wouldn't even have to buy one drink. You're so nice and the Southern girls are so nasty to their men. There's no competition. Just do it."

"I'd miss me mam," she said. The chief engineer's son sighed.

"Well, find an exceptionally nice guy and he might build a granny flat onto his five bedroomed Victorian semi."

"Don't make fun of me," she said.

"I'm not," he replied. "It's just so frustrating the way none of you ever listen, and then, by the time you're thirty-five, you're grandmothers and on about sixty a day and living on social security."

"But what am I going to do about Warren?" she said. The chief engineer's son sighed again.

"Do you love him?" he said.

"I think so," she replied.

"Do you want to spend the rest of your life with him?" he asked her.

"It won't be the rest of my life will it," she said. "Because he won't be home all the time."

"You never know," he said. "Sometimes they get the idea that they don't want to be at sea anymore and suddenly you find you're married to a security guard and all that disposable cash swishing around is gone. Then what you going to do eh? No toys for the kiddies." He reached an arm out to her, and she looked at him intently.

"I really love Warren," she said and then she pursed her lips ready for a kiss.

The chief engineer's son sat up afterwards and pondered the situation while she slept at his side looking beautiful and angelic, if very slightly overweight. He wasn't frightened of Warren. He had a black belt in Taekwondo and Warren wasn't one of those psychopathic merchant seaman who would just smash the back of your head in with a chipping hammer. I wonder why I just don't take her, he thought. I give the lecture out about how much nicer Northern girls are and how they would be snapped up in London, and then I don't snap one up myself. I'm chained to the idea that I'm under an obligation to provide a house and a Renault Five for some Southern girl who's going to lecture me on my shortcomings for the next fifty years and expect me to buy designer clothes for her kids and pay ridiculous school fees just so they can look down on me when they're older. The chief engineer's son was studying sociology in his spare time in preparation for university. Predestination, he thought. Simple conditioning, that's all.

He pulled the sheet down to look at Roxanne fully. She was so nice. Imagine that his father thought he would choose a life of those horrible women in those bars over the bliss of this. Maybe he was going round the twist, losing his mind as well as his hearing. One whispered half-joke one side of the world and it'd caused a harmless old man over here months of worry.

He stroked Roxanne. Warren definitely didn't deserve her. He wasn't strong enough to say to the others, no I don't want to come out with you, and he wasn't strong enough to say to her stay at home, either. Captain Thompson clearly liked him, but Captain Thompson clearly liked being a father figure and Warren was his latest protégée. He wondered what Captain Thompson would do when all this came out. Treat it as none of his business. Maybe. Probably. He wouldn't want to hurt him anyway. He wouldn't want to upset his father. Captains didn't like to upset their chief engineers. Their terror of the engine room meant that they always wanted to stay friends with the witch doctor who made it all work. Would his father be ashamed of him. He didn't know. How could he predict the attitude of a man whom he didn't know.

What can I do for my father, he thought. Nothing. He could tell him, listen Dad, we don't need this big money anymore. I'm just about to go to university, you and Mum have everything you could ever want, the house is paid for, you can get your retirement pension early. But his father would die. He would just sit at home and fade away, and then, one day, he would quietly die.

Warren and Roxanne were in the other joint, their home from home since Thompson had been banned from Maggie's and the others followed him. "Why do we always have to meet here Warren?" she asked him. He was silent. "You feel you'd be missing out on something if you weren't here don't you," she continued. His jaw hung open while he thought of something to say. "I came to see you Warren, not them," she said, flicking her head in the direction of his shipmates. Would you rather I hadn't come?"

"Don't be silly," he said.

"It's not being silly Warren," she told him. "Not if it's true." She pursed her lips. "You just want a white woman around occasionally?" she asked him."

"Roxanne," he said pleadingly.

"What? You don't want them to hear?" she said. "I know you're not faithful to me when I'm not around. If you don't want me, tell me. I can have others you know."

"Yeah, other unemployed people," he said.

"Don't think that's true anymore Warren," she said. "Anyway, maybe someone unemployed would be better if he were around."

"Are you faithful to me?" he asked. She blushed.

"So you admit you've been unfaithful," she said. He didn't reply. "Warren, why didn't you become an engineer?" she asked him. "Then at least you could have worked ashore if you wanted to."

"They're not real engineers," he said. "They're mechanics. If they go ashore they only get jobs as hospital maintenance men, unless they become superintendents or go and standby new builds or something, and then they're never at home either, and they don't get any long leaves, and they don't get paid much, and they're always under stress from people like Terry."

"Who's Terry?" she asked him.

"The boss," he said. "And he is evil."

"Is he fair?" she asked him.

"Not at all. Captain Roly is in prison because of him and he doesn't care. He won't even get him a decent lawyer."

"But that's irrelevant," she said. "What I want to know is what you think about us." Warren was confused. He had been an eighteen-year old deck cadet, she had been a wide-eyed fifteen-year-old Shields girl and now it seemed like she was wiser than he was and giving him the third degree. One trip abroad and she had everything sussed out. "Arc you faithful to me Warren?" she said.

"I love you," he told her.

"That's not the same thing Warren," she replied. He sighed with exasperation.

"What do you want me to tell you?" he asked her.

"Warren, I don't want you to become one of them," she said.

"I always was going to be one of them," he told her. "I was a trainee one of them when we met."

"You don't send me any money," she said. "That's the difference. Their wives put up with it because they want the money."

"So you want the money?" he said.

"That's not what I said Warren," she replied, exasperated herself now.

"When we're married, I'll send you the money," he said. "And pay the bills."

"I don't know if I want to get married anymore," she said. "I don't know if you want me. You could have told that nice captain you wanted to take me away for a few days somewhere. He would have said yes."

"That nice captain," said Warren spluttering.

"He looks after you Warren," she said. "He cares about you. I can see it. You're his favourite."

"You don't know the truth about him," said Warren.

"Go on then, tell me," she replied.

"His daughter committed suicide and now he's St Francis of Assisi. Before that he was an out and out bastard."

"I bet he was very professional," she said.

"Yeah, but still," said Warren. "Listen, let's go to your hotel if you want to be alone with me."

"That's not going to solve anything," she replied.

"What is there to solve," he said. "We're just going round and round in circles."

"I don't want to," she said.

"You just said you wanted to be alone with me," he told her.

"That's not what I meant Warren, and you know it," she said.

"So now who doesn't want whom?" he asked her.

"Warren, you're not listening," she said.

"How about if I bought you a ring?" he asked her.

"A ring would probably cost you less than one of these hookers," she said sadly.

"I can't win, can I?" he told her.

"A ring is just money," she said.

"So," he told her, "you don't want to go to your hotel with me, you don't want a ring, what do you want?"

"I want you to..." she looked around the room. "To reform," she said.

"I can't," he told her. "Not because I don't want to, but because there's nothing to reform. Listen, in ten years, I can be a supply boat captain or something; month on, month off; nice house, nice car," and after a pause, "nice little car for you."

"Thanks for the thought," she said. "Thanks for the little car."

"How any of your friends have got their own car?" he asked her.

"Warren!" she shouted, "I don't care about little cars." Some of his shipmates turned round.

"Shhh," he said quietly.

"Oh, what's the point," she said. "What is the point."

"Come on," he said soothingly. "Let's go to your hotel."

"I don't want to," she said.

"You want to stay here?" he asked with a smile.

"Maybe I want to go alone," she said.

"What," he replied, "you came halfway round the world to go to your hotel on your own." She looked at the table.

"O.K.," she said.

Thompson watched them walk out. Silly fool, he thought. I warned him. They never listen. They don't ever listen. He thought of his daughter. I could have saved your life, he said to himself, if I'd tried.

The new second engineer ran his finger along his black, military style, moustache and flexed his muscles. Years of rugby had honed them and he always flexed them when he looked around with his arrogant glare. The agent's boy dashed up to him. "Sir," he said, "you for ship." The new second engineer nodded and followed him out of arrivals through the jostling taxi-drivers, slung his bag in the opened boot, and got in the front. "You don't want sit back?" asked the agent surprised.

"In the front," said the second engineer. The agent shrugged.

"This afternoon, I will bring old second engineer airport," he said.

"No handover then," said the new second engineer.

"What?" said the agent.

"Nothing," said the new second engineer.

"He very nice guy, I like him," said the agent.

"I don't care whom you like and whom you don't like," said the second engineer. The agent looked confused. He wasn't used to dealing with unfriendly people.

"But chief engineer, he really nice guy," he said.

"He should be, he's useless, he's got to have something going for him," said the second engineer. The agent's frown increased. He really didn't understand. He turned to the second engineer again. "Listen, I'm tired, just drive," said the second engineer, and the agent gave up and just drove.

The lady journalist was getting bored with Thompson and Roly. Roly's situation dragged on too long and she was tired of Thompson's rough ways. The smooth younger men she went with back in London didn't seem so bad now even though they plastered themselves in perfume that was sold as a manly product on the basis that it had a few half-naked homosexuals on the box, and spent more time worrying about their hair than she did.

Thompson was an adventure, but she was a foreign journalist; she'd had adventure. There was a young local boy eyeing her from a table across the cafe and she caught herself smiling. The boy seemed uncertain as to whether he should approach her. Why shouldn't she do it, she thought. Thompson and his kind did it all the time. She gave him a deliberate look which could either frighten him off or be taken as an invitation, just out of curiosity. The boy took it as an invitation and was over at her side in a nanosecond.

Thompson sat down and wondered what he was going to do. The radio officer had just been beaten up in jail, Roly was apparently even sicker and there was little hope of anyone helping out. The sergeant was still being intransigent about taking a bribe over the radio officer, the lady journalist wouldn't move on Roly until that was swept away, he couldn't really get his hands on enough money to sort anything out until he got home, and if he got home with some excuse to the company, when they sent him to a ship, they wouldn't send him back here. They'd want him far away where he'd stop trying to interfere. The British consul couldn't or wouldn't help and there was no further way to force him. The man hadn't frightened long-term and carrying through with his threats would just cause more confusion and not help because the foreign office would simply replace him with someone else who was neither interested in helping nor able to help. He decided to go to see the lady journalist.

In the room, she was writhing with the local boy, her moans growing louder and louder, until finally she lay back, panting for breath. When she opened her eyes, the boy was looking at her. She smiled, but he just climbed out of bed and began to pull his jeans on. She admired the angles in his face. He really was very handsome. She smiled again, but the boy just looked at her stonily. "Hundred dollar," he said. She was shocked and then outraged. "Hundred dollar," he repeated.

"Get out of here or I tell police you raped me," she said.

"Hundred dollar!" he shouted. She started to wonder. Would the police believe her. Was it worth the bother. Suppose it got into the papers. Her lips pursed and then she climbed out of bed, took a hundred dollars out of her handbag, and gave it to him. He checked it, shoved it into his jeans pocket and left.

She was humiliated. In her day, she'd been gorgeous and used her looks to get to the top. She was a talented journalist, but so were many others, and being beautiful had tipped it for her. And she still had boys leering at her. That young boy of Thompson's for example. To think that she'd actually paid for it.

Down below, Thompson stood in a daze. He'd just been entering her hotel when he'd heard her moans from her open window above the entrance. He watched the handsome boy march out of the entrance, his head held high.

He wondered what to do: go up there and comfort her and use it as an in to get another session; or go away, let her recover from her humiliation and embarrassment, and come back when she needed to prove to herself that she was still desirable for herself alone by sleeping with him again. It was a tricky decision. He decided on the former.

He knocked on her door. "It's Thompson," he said. She opened the door, naked, and went over to the bed and got in. "You all right?" he said. She didn't answer and he went over to the side of the bed and stroked her hair. "O.K., sweetie," he murmured.

"Just get in," she said. He climbed into bed without undressing, and lay behind her with his arms wrapped around her. "It's O.K, sweetie," he said.

The new second engineer stood outside the engine control room staring at the chief engineer through the plexiglass. He had a look of studied contempt on his face and then a flicker of a smile flashed over it. He swung the door open and the chief engineer looked up at him nervously. "Hi Phil," he said. The second engineer said nothing, just moved over to the control panel and stood next to him looking at the dials. After a suitable interval calculated to show that he did not want to be friends with the chief engineer, he asked him which units were due to be done and when. The chief engineer didn't quite hear him and the second engineer sighed with sarcastic indulgence and repeated himself.

The chief engineer was intimidated. Phil had, so far as was known, never actually hit anyone but he'd made it plain that he was prepared to. He said little and everything he did was menacing, apart from when he mentioned his daughters whom he doted on as did all bullies.

The chief wished he'd asked Thompson to ask Terry not to send Phil but he knew Terry would just have laughed and he also knew that Phil was a better engineer than himself, that the company did not consider him to be a good engineer and that they had probably deliberately assigned Phil to the ship to compensate for his being the chief engineer.

"Phil..." he said, starting a sentence during which he planned to ask for cooperation, but then, when Phil turned to face him, he thought better of it. He wondered if Phil would embarrass him in front of his son by belittling him.

The trouble with bullies, thought the chief engineer, was that if one gave in, which he had, there was no end to it. Things just got worse and worse. The only option open to him was to slam a chipping hammer into his head but he was not a killer like some, and this ship was not going to sea and there was no way of getting rid of the body. Dump it in the harbour, and it would just float about until it was found.

The chief left the engine room and went up onto the main deck and found Thompson hanging over the rail on the companionway. "So, how's Phil?" said Thompson. He had no idea that the chief was frightened of Phil, not being frightened of him himself.

"Fine," said the chief.

"He'll sort some things out," said Thompson.

"I'm sure he will," said the chief sadly.

"What's wrong?" said Thompson.

"Nothing," said the chief.

"Is your son with Warren's girl?" he asked him. The chief recoiled in horror.

"What?" he said. Thompson laughed.

"It'll do Warren good anyway. He's far too nice and naive. That'll let him know what the world, and especially women, are really like."

"My son is..." said the chief.

"Honourable?" said Thompson.

"He is a fine young man," said the chief. "Better man than me," I think. Thompson slapped him playfully on the upper arm.

112

"What you talking about?" he said. "What's he done with his life yet. You're a chief engineer. He strikes me as one of those types who gets a nice high-paying job in the media and then waffles on and on about socialism. Don't know why you ever worried about his getting a job in the merchant navy. He is not like us at all. He's totally not suited."

"He's not soft you know," said the chief. Thompson snorted. "Really, he's not," said the chief. "My wife's brothers; they were all tough. He takes after them."

"Looks like you could blow him over," said Thompson.

"Don't be fooled," said the chief.

Phil appeared behind them, his ear defenders hanging around his neck. He didn't plan on going deaf like the chief, and even the generators made a hell of a noise.

"Captain," said Phil in greeting.

"How you doing Phil?" said Thompson.

"Fine," said the second engineer.

"The chief brought you up to speed?" said Thompson. The chief's face flushed.

Yeah, sure," said Phil. He smiled slightly and Thompson looked at him, and then Phil turned and went away.

"I've never understood that man," he said to the chief. The chief said nothing. "I said I've never understood him," said Thompson again.

"I don't like him," said the chief.

"Cheer up," said Thompson, after a moment. "At least he'll fix everything," he continued.

"Because I can't?" said the chief.

"I didn't say that," said Thompson. "I didn't mean it either." He slapped him on the back. "Come on me old matey. Where's the guy I went up the road with in Singapore when we were sixteen?"

"He died?" said the chief.

"He died," scoffed Thompson. "What are you on about?"

"I'd better go back down the engine room," said the chief. "I suppose Phil will be down soon to tell me exactly how we're going to be running things."

"He's not so bad," said Thompson to his departing figure.

"I hate him," said the chief over his shoulder.

Thompson pondered this. He'd heard people talking about Phil for years. Some people liked him, some people didn't but the ones who didn't always moaned about him quietly. Not being a man who'd ever been frightened, Thompson had difficulty recognising fear in other people.

Captain was a strange job, he thought. He spent half his time being a kind of social worker which seeing as he despised social workers was quite ironic. He wondered if he could have ever done another job. An office would have been suffocating. A simple menial job would have been too boring for him. If you were to compress all the time he'd spent with his wife over the last thirty years you'd find that he'd only been with her for a solid seven or eight. Family life passing him by. That was the source of his sadness and sense of loss.

I missed my daughter's childhood, he thought, and she never had an adulthood. There was the regret. But what was the answer, suicide himself? He enjoyed life, dealing with one situation after another, never knowing what was coming. So he moped. Didn't mean he wasn't having fun.

He looked at the sparkling blue water, sighed and threw his cigarette over the side.

The lady journalist was packing when Thompson entered her hotel room. "What are you doing?" he said.

"What does it look like?" she replied.

"But you can't go. What about Roly?" he said.

She turned to face him and cocked her head to one side and said, "Your friend is going to die in prison and I don't see what my hanging around here being humiliated is going to achieve."

"What are you talking about?" said Thompson.

"You know what I'm talking about," she replied. Thompson looked at her desperately.

"I can't count the number of times a woman went with me and I thought she liked me and then she asked for money," he said.

"That's different, you're not a woman," she said. She sighed. "Listen." she told him. "You don't really think he's getting out do you. He's been abandoned by your company, by the Government, by everyone."

"Not quite everyone," said Thompson.

"All right, everyone apart from you," she said.

"Come on, we've got to keep trying," said Thompson. "I thought you liked it here. What are you going to do if you get back to London? You've got the rest of your life to spend in that dump."

"I don't want to be a laughing stock," she said.

"Who's laughing?" said Thompson. "No one knows."

"Your friend Maggie will know," she said, "and she will tell everyone."

"So what," said Thompson exasperated. "I thought you lady journalists were tough. You get shot at, get raped, you just keep going."

"You took advantage of me when I was humiliated," she said. Thompson threw his arms open wide.

"We've had sex lots of times."

"Yes, but I needed support," she said.

"I thought you were tough," said Thompson. "You're just another whining professional feminist. You've got a chance to actually do something good here. You could save a man's life."

"Don't be dramatic," she said.

"I think a good man being beaten and starved to death in a third world prison is quite dramatic, don't you?" he said. She sat down on the bed.

"I told you, my editor won't do anything while that paedophile is still in jail. You have to make all that go away."

"I'm working on it," he said. "The sergeant says he will take a bribe; then he says he won't; then he says he will; then he lowers the amount; then he raises the amount."

"Get to the girl then. Tell your friend Maggie to sort her out."

"I tried. Maggie threw me out of her place and won't speak to me anymore," he said.

"A whore with principles," she said.

"Maggie doesn't have any principles," said Thompson, she's just scared of the sergeant." He brightened up. "You could just do an article on the general life of this town while you're waiting for developments in Roly's case," he said. "You know, interviews with the locals, the sinister air etc… etc... The Economist does it all the time. Your paper could too."

"You really don't know anything do you," she said. "apart from how much a prostitute costs in each port and how to get a big ship from A to B." Thompson shrugged.

"That's more than most people," he said. They both laughed. He went over and sat at her side. "Come on," he said. She pursed her lips.

"I can give it a little bit longer," she said. "But I have to go soon," you know. "I'm a salaried person. "I can't just hang around here indefinitely." Thompson knew that he'd won a reprieve. The bustling sound of the street and the creaking fan provided a soundtrack to their little contemplations. Finally, he said, "What was it like, with the boy?"

"You know what it was like, you were listening," she said.

"Yeah," said Thompson.

Thompson stood with Phil on the main deck, looking out at the valves and pipelines. "You could kill her," said Phil. "Or him."

"I'm not a killer," said Thompson.

"I don't mean yourself," said Phil.

"I'm still not a killer," said Thompson. "Even if I get someone to do it for me, it's the same thing."

"Except you can't be caught," said Phil.

I don't want to do that," said Thompson. "I don't want to have some innocent girl killed."

"She's not innocent, she set him up," said Phil.

"She probably didn't have any choice," said Thompson.

"Kill him then," said Phil.

"What's the point in killing one of my guys to save another one," said Thompson exasperated.

"He's a paedophile," said Phil. Phil, having daughters, was very self-righteous when confronted with this kind of thing.

"He isn't a paedophile," said Thompson. "He's just an arrogant little twerp."

"You ask me my advice, and then you just tell me I'm wrong," said Phil.

"Yeah, yeah, I'm sorry," said Thompson. Whenever Thompson said sorry, it always sounded as though he was spitting out glass. "How you getting on with the chief?" he said, suddenly.

"He's an idiot and totally incompetent," said Phil.

"He's a nice guy," said Thompson, " and there aren't many nice guys around."

"If you're in a job, you should be able to do that job," said Phil.

"Well, you could do your chief's and then the company would make you a chief," said Thompson. "You can't have it both ways. You can't not want the responsibility and then knock someone who's prepared to take it on."

"If you're in a job, you should be able to do the job," insisted Phil.

Thompson knew the truth, Phil wasn't sure that he would pass his chief's technical exams and feared humiliation. The fact that no one would laugh at him even if he did fail, didn't matter to him. So, he just sat back and used his superior engineering skills to humiliate nice guy chiefs. Thompson tried to remember if anyone had ever hit Phil. He didn't think so. Someone should have but like all bullies, Phil was careful to avoid picking on anyone who might be a genuine threat." Phil blinked in the sunlight.

"Kill them both," he said and then he laughed and moved off down the deck.

Thompson sat opposite the radio officer. This place was grim, even grimmer than Roly's jail. "You're going to kill me aren't you," said the radio officer, "to save Roly." Thompson shook his head in astonishment.

"No, of course not. I'm trying to bribe the sergeant to let everything go but he keeps upping the amount, and it's difficult to get the deal over with. Your mother wants to help."

"The company should help," said the radio officer.

"The company won't help Roly and he was more or less following their instructions," said Thompson.

"The consul should help," said the radio officer.

"Well, he thinks you were guilty so what will he do?" replied Thompson.

"You threatened him over Roly," said the radio officer.

"As I keep saying," said Thompson, "Roly is a different matter.

"So what's going to happen to me?" said the radio officer. Thompson shrugged.

"You just stay here for the foreseeable future I suppose." He looked around him and then back at the radio officer. "Why did you do it?" he said.

"Stubbornness," said the radio officer.

"Ten years ago, no one would have even known what the problem was," said Thompson. "Times change."

The guard was looking agitated and indicating that they should wind it up. Thompson rose. "Take care of yourself. Don't give up yet," he said.

Outside the prison gates, Thompson wondered if he were a killer. Could he have some innocent thirteen-year-old girl killed. It would be easy to do here. His role would be unlikely to come out. She would just disappear. He could tell himself that she was evil and deserved it but he knew that she'd just been manipulated or threatened the same as Roly: just another victim of circumstances. He decided to try to see her. If he couldn't bribe the sergeant, maybe he could bribe her.

At the agent's office, the chairman and Terry were shouting at him down the phone. "You told her that the company leaned on him!" said Terry. Thompson could just hear the chairman in the background saying, "Tell him he's fired." He knew they wouldn't. That would give the lady journalist more ammunition.

"You did lean on him," said Thompson.

"The captain has supreme command," said Terry.

"Hah," said Thompson, "that went out with Captain Cook." He could almost picture Terry's face turning bright red and the chairman's eyebrows meeting in the middle of his forehead, his face squeezed in fury.

"The company bears no responsibility," said Terry.

"I'm too old to listen to threats," said Thompson.

"Who's threatening you?" said Terry exasperated. "There you go again. No one threatened you, you're just making that up."

"I heard the chairman saying, "Fire him,"" said Thompson. Then he heard the chairman saying, "He can't prove that."

"I'm very surprised at your attitude," said Terry.

"Oh give over," said Thompson, "that's what personnel girls say when they get any lip from teenage cadets. Listen, either fire me or leave me alone to do my job."

"I advise you that slander against the company will not be tolerated," said Terry. "By the time our lawyers have finished with you, we'll own your house."

"I don't own it now," said Thompson, "the wife owns it. The judge gave it to her."

"We'll take it from her then," said Terry furiously.

"Listen, I don't care what you do," said Thompson, "but you get Roly out or it's going to get messier and messier. Negotiate some big insurance payout and give it to the government here or something. Just settle for crew negligence. Who cares. The chairman will still be able to afford horse-riding lessons for Penelope and Jemima." He heard the chairman saying, "Give me that," and trying to wrestle the receiver out of Terry's hands. "Anything more?" said Thompson. There was silence. "Good," he finished and put the receiver back in its cradle. He looked up at the agent, who seemed to be highly amused.

"I never hear captain talk to office like that," he said.

"Yeah, well," said Thompson, when you're at the end of your rope you don't care too much anymore."

Thompson went up the steps to the girl's house and knocked on the wooden door. A woman who looked about sixty, but was probably nearer forty, answered and opened up. Thompson glared at her and then moved her aside and walked in. He saw the radio officer's girl sitting at the kitchen table.

He thought she might try to run, but she didn't. She just sat staring at him. He slumped down in a chair opposite her.

"Come on," he said, "how much?"

"I can't," she said, "the sergeant will send me to jail."

"You could take the money and go away," said Thompson.

"He will find me," she said.

"How old were you when you lost your virginity?" he asked idly.

"Thirteen," she said. Thompson thought he'd love to bring this up as the lawyer in court. "Milord, this girl has been a professional prostitute since the age of thirteen, she was not some innocent flower corrupted by my client." He imagined what such thoughts bandied about back home would cost him, a file at the police station and a shunning by the community perhaps. "It's no good captain," she said. "I didn't want to do it. Maggie and the sergeant made me. My sister is already in jail. The sergeant is evil. He doesn't care. You know what he did to my friend. He locked her up all night in the men's cell and let the other guards watch."

"Yeah, I heard about that," said Thompson.

"Your friend best kill himself," she said. "If he do not, other prisoners will soon."

"Oh God," said Thompson.

"Captain, you a good man, you want help your friend. You cannot help him. He not good man. I don't know why you care." No, he isn't a good man, thought Thompson, but in order to help another man who is a good man, I first have to help him.

Phil was looking at the chief as if he were a piece of dirt. "I spent all yesterday changing those seals," he said, "not to mention the cost to the company." The chief stood looking forlornly at the water maker which he'd just blown, through starting it up with the wrong valves shut.

"It's on the list to check," he said.

"On the list to check, not to break, you idiot," said Phil. "You really are useless do you know that." This was true, but it wasn't the chief's fault that the company had kept him on too long, and he'd been trying to work rather than just sitting in his cabin like half the chiefs in the company.

"I'll rebuild it," he said.

"We don't have any more seals you useless bastard," said Phil. This was really too much. Someone should have smashed Phil's face in years ago but everybody was intimidated.

The chief looked at the engine room bottom plates. At this point a softer man might have said something like, "Oh well, never mind," but not Phil. He just glared at the chief.

"I don't know why Thompson likes you," he said.

"We go back a long way," said the chief quietly.

"Lucky for you," said Phil. The chief wondered why he didn't just pick up an adjustable spanner and smash it into Phil's face but he knew why. He was just too gentle a person.

Suddenly Phil became aware that there was someone behind him. He saw too the look on the chief's face. Turning, he found himself looking at the chief's son. Phil stared at him, but he was puzzled. The chief's son was just a kid but he didn't have that look of fear which Phil was so accustomed to seeing in other people. He didn't even look nervous. How long has he been standing there, he wondered. He turned back to the chief. "Just leave it," he said and then he walked out of the engine room.

The chief's son raised an eyebrow. The chief just pursed his lips.

Thompson was with his mama-san lover. "Is there anything you can do?" he asked her. She shook her head.

"I told you," she answered him. "Maggie's doing. How is your white lady?"

"I am only with her because I think she can help Captain Roly," he said.

"I do not believe this," she replied.

"What do you care anyway?" said Thompson. "You are a professional. As soon as I am gone you will be with another captain."

"I prefer chief engineers," she said. "At least they can fix things." She pointed to her broken ceiling fan. "Captains are useless."

"You obviously haven't met my chief," said Thompson quietly.

"What will you do when the fight happens?" she said.

"What fight?" asked Thompson mystified.

"The fight between your pet boy and the son of the chief engineer?"

"Warren is not my pet boy," said Thompson. "Anyway, how comes everyone knows about this?"

"The hotel staff," said the mama-san.

"Of course," said Thompson. "It's not a problem, Warren is not violent. Anyway, better he finds out now what she is like."

"She nice girl," said the mama-san. Warren, he go with bad girls while she here. He to blame."

"Did he really?" said Thompson shocked. "The silly fool."

"She nice girl," said the mama-san. "I could make money out of her." Thompson laughed.

"You're all heart," he said.

"I'm sorry about your friend Roly," said the mama-san. I remember him from years ago. He very nice guy but he dead man. Best forget. Your government no care. Your company no care."

People brought up in poverty had such a practical view of the world thought Thompson. "How is lady journalist in bed?" she asked, changing the subject abruptly. "I hear she very good."

"Oh God," said Thompson, "you know about that."

"Everybody know," said the mama-san. "Once, we had a lady pay the boys. She was French, so we didn't think too much of it, but this lady English."

"She didn't know," said Thompson, "not that I'm admitting anything."

"That's what your radio officer said," she observed.

"Oh God, he wasn't underage was he," said Thompson.

"No, he is twenty-five," she told him. Relax."

"He's a relative of yours isn't he," said Thompson, " a ray of light suddenly penetrating his brain. The mama-san smiled.

"He is my cousin," she said. "That lady had pride. It had to be burst."

"Punctured," said Thompson.

"What?" she said.

"You puncture pride, you don't burst it," he said.

"Now she pays men for sex. I never did that," she said. "None of my girls ever did that."

"Yeah, yeah," said Thompson.

"You went with her over me because I am a hooker, but she worse than a hooker. She is a hooker who can't even get sex without paying herself."

"I told you," said Thompson, I went with her because I thought she might be able to help my friend.

"Liar," said the mama-san.

The lady journalist sat with Roxanne at the breakfast table. "Do you think Warren is loyal?" said Roxanne.

"Not a chance," said the lady journalist. But neither are you, are you, judging from the noise through the partition the other night.

"That wasn't the same," said Roxanne. "He tricked me."

"How?" said the lady journalist.

"He pretended to be sympathetic," said Roxanne.

"He probably was sympathetic. Anyway, you're too young to be getting into a serious relationship with someone who's away for so long. That's for women who've had their fun."

"But Warren...," said Roxanne.

"Warren, Warren, Warren," said the lady journalist. "I don't even like the name. It's not a proper man's name is it, like Fred, or Bill or Ron." She remembered Warren's eyes being all over her naked body. "At least you can be sure he's not gay," she said.

"What?" said Roxanne confused.

"Nothing," said the lady journalist.

Thompson sat in the little booth in front of Roly again. Roly was out of the prison hospital now.

"You know the complications don't you?" he said. Roly was quiet. "Come on," said Thompson.

"What are you thinking?" said Roly. Thompson flicked his finger across his throat. Roly twisted in torment. "Her or him?" he said. Thompson's brow furrowed.

"Her," he said.

"Don't do it," said Roly. Thompson bit his lip. "You're not a killer and she's just a girl."

"She set the radio officer up," said Thompson. "She's a little bitch."

"There's no certainty I'll get out anyway," said Roly. "It's just that this newspaper will push a bit. The only one who's certain to benefit is your girlfriend. She'll get a byline. That's why she's keen, not because she cares about me."

"Who cares why she wants to do it," said Thompson, exasperated. "I care about you."

"You'll do it or someone else?" said Roly.

"Someone else," said Thompson.

"I won't last much longer anyway," said Roly. "It's a waste of time."

"Don't give up," said Thompson.

"I had a letter from my wife's lawyer," said Roly. Thompson was surprised.

"She wants a divorce?" he said.

"Oh no, nothing like that. She wants to make sure the will is all in order," he said. "See, she thinks I won't be around much longer."

"Bitch," said Thompson.

"I thought she loved me once," said Roly.

"Thirty or forty years ago," said Thompson.

"You've never killed anyone have you?" said Roly. "Never done a chipping hammer in the skull thing and thrown the body over the side?"

"No," said Thompson quietly.

"What makes you think you won't go to pieces with the guilt?" said Roly. "Then you'll be in here, and I'll be out. What will be the point in that? I don't think you could do it anyway. I don't think you've got it in you to kill someone." He saw

Thompson was about to interrupt. "Yeah, yeah, or have them killed," he continued.

"She's just another third-world hooker," said Thompson.

"You say that now but you'll feel guilty," said Roly.

"For a while," said Thompson.

"Maybe I deserve to be in here?" said Roly.

"Come on, you were doing what the company wanted," said Thompson. "Why should you be in here when all those government paedophiles and merchant bankers stealing widows and orphans pension funds receive knighthoods."

"That's life isn't it?" said Roly.

"You don't want any help, but I'm going to do it anyway," said Thompson.

"No you won't," said Roly.

"I will," said Thompson.

"How are the boys?" said Roly.

"Your sons?" said Thompson.

"No, the A.B.s," said Roly.

"Fine," said Thompson. "They're in their own country, course they're happy. They're very apologetic about what happened to you. They can't bribe every single prison gang, and the one they did just wasn't watching for a moment and..."

"Yeah, yeah, they tried," said Roly.

"I wonder if they would have fired you if you'd just refused to dump it," said Thompson.

"Terry would have fired me in a nanosecond," said Roly, "and he would have done everything in his power to screw up my pension."

"Anyway, it doesn't do any good to brood on that," said Thompson.

"So why bring it up?" said Roly. Thompson flushed. He felt foolish.

"Sorry," he said.

"It's all right, I'm grateful you came all the way to see me again," said Roly. "Just don't do, you know, kill her."

"Yeah, yeah," said Thompson.

"How's Maggie," asked Roly.

"Bitch," said Thompson. "You know she was in on it."

"Yeah, yeah, it's just business though," said Roly. "nothing personal."

"You are the most charitable man on the planet," said Thompson. "You even want to forgive the girl who put the man in jail that caused..." he saw Roly's face and stopped talking.

"You don't think I'll do it, do you?" he said. Roly smiled and shook his head.

"I will," said Thompson. "You're my only friend."

"Make new friends," said Roly.

"Too difficult," said Thompson.

"Think of yourself," said Roly. "Don't put yourself through all this."

"My wife treats me like a charity case," said Thompson. "She makes me feel like a little boy on the phone."

"You need to get drunk and get in a fight," said Roly. Thompson looked up at him.

"You've always seemed so placid to me," he said. "All through all these years, I often wondered how you did it."

"You always seemed excessively violent to me," said Roly.

"It costs nothing to have someone killed here," said Thompson. "I can easily organise it. The thing is if you do someone like this, don't talk about it yourself. I go that from some gangland acquaintance."

"You won't be able to stop yourself," said Roly. "You'll probably blurt it all out to your wife and she'll call the police. They'll just love that. They can pass the information on, claim all the credit, and let the local police do all the work and the British Government can look like good international citizens by handing you over and I'll be even more firmly in here. They might as well weld the cell door shut." Thompson laughed and then Roly laughed too.

"I'm still going to do it," said Thompson abruptly.

"No, you're still not," said Roly.

Thompson looked at the man who sat with him in the bar. It wasn't either of the mama-sans' bars, it was an out of the way place. The man looked bored. Thompson didn't know whether that was a good sign or not.

"She just disappear," said Thompson. The man nodded. Thompson wondered if he even spoke English.

"You sure Captain?" he asked him, confirming that he did.

"She's the cause of all our problems," said Thompson. The man snorted.

"Company cause of problem," he replied.

"Yes, well," said Thompson.

"She die painfully, she pay," said the man. Thompson sighed. He didn't want to know all this. The man just didn't understand.

"Not necessary," he said. "She just disappear." He wondered why it was different because it was a girl. He was sure he could arrange a man's death without any feeling, though he never had. "I don't want her to die, I just want her to disappear," he said. He had to be careful. He was just covering himself but he wanted the man to understand what he really meant.

"She disappear," said the man. Thompson looked down at his drink. I'm evil, he thought.

The chief engineer stood alongside him in Thompson's mama-san's place. "Don't do it," he said.

"Don't do what," said Thompson in shock.

"Whatever you're planning, don't do it," said the chief engineer. Thompson looked at him his mouth wide open. "I've known you more than thirty years," said the chief. "You always look like this when you're about to do something stupid. Listen, honestly, I'm sure it'll have something to do with those two idiots. But the radio officer deserves it, and Roly wants to die, he's had enough."

"How can you say that?" said Thompson.

"It's the truth," said the chief.

"He's only in his fifties," said Thompson.

"He wants to die," said the chief.

"Well, I've heard of Scottish…," said Thompson.

"Scottish what?" said the chief.

"Scottish…," said Thompson. The chief suddenly appeared nervous. Phil was staring at him from the other side of the room. Thompson followed his eyes, saw Phil and smiled. Thompson thought Phil was a great guy because Phil being a bully and Thompson being tough, Phil didn't pick on him or let him see him picking on anyone else. Thompson turned to look at the chief. As far as he was concerned, the chief should be grateful that he had someone decent to look out for him and prevent his own uselessness causing a disaster.

From another corner of the room, the chief's son was staring at Phil, breaking away from his conversation with Roxanne and Warren. Warren still hadn't found out that anything had happened between Roxanne and the chief's son. The crew knew from the hotel staff but thought it better to keep the information to themselves.

Phil walked over to the chief and Thompson, and the chief flinched. "How's it going?" Phil said cheerfully, looking at Thompson.

"All right Phil?" said Thompson. "Sorted the engine room out yet?" he asked him. He laughed. "Only joking," he said, digging the chief in the ribs.

"It's just perfect," said Phil sarcastically. It was strange about Phil. He hated sarcasm in other people but used it himself all the time.

Thompson saw the chief's son staring at Phil and was puzzled. He wondered what was going on. Had Phil been with Roxanne. That wasn't Phil's style. He'd never known him go with anyone. He was a loyal husband and father type. And Roxanne wasn't like that. She's just slipped up with the chief's son. Easy, he supposed, for a girl from a Northern council estate to fall for someone so well-spoken and suave and public-schooly as the chief's son.

"Where's your lady friend?" said Phil.

"Writing some communiqué," said Thompson. "She'll have to go home soon."

"She's freelance, she can stay as long as she likes," said Phil.

"She's salaried," said Thompson. "I can't support her, thanks to that gay judge who gave my wife everything."

"How do you know he was gay?" said Phil, taking Thompson's words literally.

"Feminist supporting then, if not gay," said Thompson. Thompson was feeling a little light-headed. It's not every day you order the murder of a young girl with everything to live for, he

140

thought. He wondered how they'd do it. They wouldn't waste any bullets. It'd be a quick slash with a machete or something.

Suddenly, an air of menace descended on the joint as the sergeant and two of his men entered. Thompson wondered if he'd been set-up. The sergeant looked straight at him and smiled. He wanted another captain in jail, thought Thompson, this time, put there by him. Imagine the publicity for the sergeant. In this country, he could run for president on the back of it. He realised the stupidity of what he'd done, but he felt he was on a moving walkway and couldn't get off. The sergeant turned and left.

The mama-san went over to Thompson and stared at him as if to say, "What have you done?" Thompson shrugged. Even Phil was looking confused.

Thompson wondered what to do. She had to die so everything else would fall into place. Did the sergeant know or not. Could he stop the killer if he wanted to. Presumably, if they got all their money, they wouldn't care. He didn't suppose their operation was loaded down with principles and mission statements.

"I thought you'd be on your own tonight," said the chief, breaking Thompson's chain of thought.

"What?" he said. "Why?" The chief looked embarrassed.

"Isn't it two years since your daughter, you know?" he replied. Thompson reddened. How could he have forgotten. Phil turned and walked away.

"She held the whole Central Line up for an hour," he said absent-mindedly." He looked like he was miles away.

"I'm sorry I reminded you," said the chief. "I thought... I mean, I just thought."

"You thought no one could forget his daughter's suicide but I did," said Thompson. "I did. I should ring the wife. No, I shouldn't. She won't care."

"She will," said the chief.

"It's all we had in common," said Thompson.

"Imagine how the father of that girl will feel?" said the chief. Thompson shot him a glance. For a man who was so useless at his job, the chief had uncanny perception, he thought. He flushed.

"I don't know what you're talking about," he said.

"Yeah, you do," said the chief. Thompson's mind stirred. It sounded like the words of someone else. He remembered. Roly's words at the jail. "Oh, you're still not," and his own words, "Yeah, I am." All these people knew him better than he knew himself. That's what a lifetime of self-deception did.

Thompson woke up sweating. He'd had a nightmare. There he was, trying to hold his daughter's hand while she flung herself out into the void in front of the onrushing tube train, and she kept slipping from his fingers. He suddenly thought, it's not like that. They just flop down off the platform in front of the wheels, but then he decided he was going mad. He felt the loss, the hopelessness and something else gnawed at him but he didn't know what and then he realised, the murder. His subconscious was telling him not to do it. Don't kill her. The chief knew. How did he know. He sensed it. It was logical. It was the ruthless move, and the chief knew he was a ruthless man.

Thompson waited for the killer in his mama-san's place. The killer came in after a while and sat down opposite him. Thompson squirmed, trying to find the right words. He was aware that the door behind him had opened again because it let in a pool of light, but he didn't turn and he didn't realise that it was the lady journalist who'd entered, and she stood behind him, pursed her lips and went through to the ladies' toilet, and he still didn't know it was her.

The killer had refused to meet him in some secret place. He'd said he was busy, and it was here or else nowhere.

Thompson whispered. "I can't do it, I don't want you to do it," he said. The killer did not look surprised, just a little annoyed. "I want the rest of the money," he said. Thompson had been hoping that he wouldn't say that but he handed it over. He wasn't about to attempt to negotiate. "And your friend?" asked the killer, "you will abandon him?"

"I'll get him out some other way," said Thompson. The killer rose up and then gave Thompson the benefit of his opinion. 'You're a stupid man," he said, and then he left.

The lady journalist came forwards from behind the door off the corridor leading to the ladies' lavatory and sat down opposite Thompson. Thompson wasn't worried. He hadn't said anything incriminating. Because he'd spent most of his life dealing with women of little intelligence or women who barely understood English he'd forgotten that there were some intelligent ones who did understand, and the lady journalist was one. "How are you?" he said. She stared at him. "What?" he said.

"You were going to kill that girl weren't you," she said.

"Are you crazy?" he asked her.

"You were," she said.

"You can't accuse me of something like that on no evidence," he said, panicking a little. She continued to stare at him. "I wasn't going to kill her," he continued.

"You were going to pay someone else, it's the same thing," she said. Thompson said nothing. She rose slowly, still staring at him. "I'm going to my hotel, I'm going to pack my things and leave. Don't follow me," she told him.

"You're crazy if you think that," he said. She turned her back on him and moved over to the door. "What do you care anyway?" he said, in frustration. "It's more of a story for you if she disappears. You don't care. If there were no starving war orphans or political prisoners or...," he couldn't think of any other worthy causes, "you'd be out of a job."

The doors flapped closed behind her.

I don't need you, he thought. I'll get him out. He realised that the lady journalist probably could not have done a lot. Her editor would have wanted her to focus on some ethnic minority activist or dissident. She'd just wanted to sleep around in the heat. Yeah, he told himself, that's all she wanted. But he didn't know for definite. Roly, he thought in despair, why didn't you just tell the company you wouldn't do it.

He waited outside her hotel, despite what she'd told him and tried to speak to her when she walked out and into the waiting taxi but she just ignored him then, when she was inside, she opened the window and said, "I'm going to buy my ticket. Leave me alone. You're lucky I don't go to the police." As he looked after the speeding vehicle, Thompson thought she was right and was alarmed. "Captain tries to have victim of rapist officer killed to protect incompetent friend." There's a story but she would have to make it known that she'd let it be known that if it weren't for the girl, she'd help. Would she do that. He didn't think so. He was relieved. It'd be all right. He just had to find another way to help Roly.

There had to be something he could do. Maybe he should lean on the consul again. Maybe Roly should just escape. Would the Labour

Government send him back. They were do-gooders. Would the public stand for some old seaman being shipped off to jail in Asia even if he had killed some fish. But Roly would never make it out of the country. He wouldn't get as far as the airport.

He went off towards the shipyard. He felt like walking. He started to think he would miss making love to the lady journalist. She had some body on her for a woman of that age. Even the male hooker had looked satisfied when he left her room.

The consul laid back on his chaise longue and puffed on his pipe while his ladyboy massaged his feet. He wasn't afraid of Thompson. He had been a Guards officer. He was just feeling that Thompson had a point. If he couldn't do anything for British subjects in trouble then what really was the point in his being here. He blew out a puff of smoke and watched it curl its way to the punkah rotating slowly in the ornate ceiling.

There was a slim chance. If he could start pulling strings and mooching, he might get something moving. London would not be happy. They didn't want to know about this. The sensible thing for him if he wanted to move up was to let sleeping dogs lie, or rather sleeping captains rot, but he didn't really feel he was ever going to get Washington so why bother tiptoeing around for the next thirty years. He sipped his cocktail and mused on his plan.

The ladyboy suddenly caught one of his nails in the consul's toe and the consul lent forward and slapped his face. "Be more careful," he said sharply. The ladyboy reddened but continued with a more studious attitude. "You wouldn't have lasted five minutes at my school," said the consul with a little smile to show that he was not really annoyed. The ladyboy giggled.

Phil approached Thompson out on the boiling deck. "So what was going on, you've been white for the past few days and that pathetic chief..."

"The chief's all right," said Thompson curtly, cutting him off." Phil looked puzzled.

"Anyway," he continued, "what's been going on."

"None of your business," said Thompson. Phil raised his eyebrows and went to move away. "I'm sorry," said Thompson. "It's just that I'm..."

"You're what?" said Phil.

"It's Roly," said Thompson, "and that other idiot."

"You're not responsible for them," said Phil. "You weren't onboard when Roly did what he did, he was his own captain, and that other guy wasn't onboard. It wasn't professional. It was his personal life."

"I know, I know," said Thompson.

"None of the other captains cares," said Phil.

"I know they don't," said Thompson. "But you don't understand." Phil shrugged and went off down the deck to the engine room stairwell.

Thompson and Roly were on the same ship in Sydney when they were teenagers, Thompson an uncertificated third officer, and Roly, a senior apprentice. The sun was hot, the work was hard and the dockers were obstreperous and uncooperative. Thompson was becoming more and more frustrated and the more frustrated he became, the more the Australians took pleasure in winding him up. They started shoving him as they moved around the derricks, just gently barging him with their shoulders.

Then the stroppiest stood up and looked him straight in the face. "That ladder ain't safe mate," he said.

"What's wrong with it?" said Thompson.

"There's oil on it," said the docker. Thompson looked at it.

"So what," he said.

"It ain't safe," said the docker.

"Wipe it up then," said Thompson. The docker raised himself to his full height. "Ain't my job," he said, with a mocking smile on his face. Thompson swore at him and likened him to a part of the female anatomy. The docker's face went bright red and his friends stopped in the little that they were doing to look at him and to see what his reaction would be. The docker stared at Thompson for thirty seconds, his cheeks pumped out, his face still red and then bent back to his work. Thompson nodded in satisfaction and moved away.

The day over, and Roly and Thompson donned their up the road gear and went down the gangway. Security was non-existent in those days and they drifted out of the docks and into their customary first stop. "I don't think we should be in here," said Roly, looking around him.

"Why?" said Thompson.

"There's all these dockers in here. Anyway, we see them all day, who wants to see them in the evening."

"We're only starting out here," said Thompson. "You worry too much." He swirled the remainder of his schooner and tipped it down his throat. "I'm the senior man here," he said jokingly." He moved away from the bar. "What is it they say here, point Percy at the porcelain?" He went over to the toilets.

He was just doing up his zip when he hear a crack and then a loud thud behind him. He turned to see the docker from that afternoon prone on the floor with blood oozing from his head and a World War II Luger in his hand. Behind him stood Roly with a shattered beer bottle in his own hand. Neither spoke, they just stood looking at each other. "I saved your life," said Roly, finally.

"You did," said Thompson.

"He had that gun pointed right at the back of your head," said Roly.

"I'm sure he did," said Thompson.

"What shall we do?" said Roly.

"Let's get out of here," said Thompson. The police might take him in and beat him up, they might not. We don't want to wait and find out."

The docker groaned and Thompson was tempted to kick him but thought better of it. He pondered his luck. Just one slight difference and he would have had the back of his head blown off by this guy with his souvenir. If Roly hadn't seen him enter after him. If Roly hadn't followed him. It didn't bear thinking about.

They sat on a terrace in another bar. "Roly," said Thompson, "if you ever need..."

"Yeah, yeah, I know," said Roly.

The lady journalist was infuriated. Roxanne stood in the doorway of her room while she threw her clothes into her suitcase. "Scumbag," said the lady journalist.

"Who?" said Roxanne, confused.

"Thompson," said the lady journalist.

"The captain?" said Roxanne.

"How many other Thompsons are there around right now?" asked the lady journalist. She had regarded Roxnne as a simpleton and this just confirmed her in her opinion.

"What's he done?" said Roxanne.

"Believe me, you don't want to know," said the journalist. She stood, hand on hip, staring at Roxanne. "Sweetie," she said, "you are too good for this lot, but do you want to know what I think?"

"Yes," said Roxanne.

"Stay with that boy Warren. Out of all of them, he's the least worst. You'll hardly ever have him around anyway and if he ever does leave you, you'll get the lot. That other one is just having fun.

He's bright and super-confident and he's going to end up with a nice blonde girl who rides ponies and whose dad made a fortune through scrap metal or something and then gained respectability by donating to charity. He's too smart for you and he's going to get bored with you if he even contacts you again once you all go home."

Roxanne looked like she was going to cry and the journalist sighed and went and put her arm around her. "I'm sorry. I'm just furious over Thompson. All my time wasted." Roxanne wiped her eyes.

"You had fun," she said. The lady journalist considered this.

"I suppose I did," she said. She picked up her case and her handbag. "Thompson's friend is going to rot in jail and so is that radio officer. They should all rot."

"My dad always said where would we be without them," said Roxanne defensively.

"Ah, he was one too was he?" said the journalist. "Well, you take your choice sweetie." She gave Roxanne a little peck on the cheek on her way out, and Roxanne blushed.

Roly sat in his cell and read the letter from his wife. It was one long complaint. There were no lines from his sons. They never supported him. They just took. He wondered if he could have produced finer sons if he'd just let them go to the local comprehensive instead of a fee-paying school. He imagined some bulky skinhead turning up in his Newcastle or Sunderland top and demanding to see him and handing over a big packet of tobacco and other goodies. If he hadn't had to pay those school fees, he could have retired five years ago.

His wife wanted to make sure his will was sorted out. She even had the cheek to mention that she'd been to see a solicitor.

It was strange. Roly had conformed. Like a lot of his kind he'd spent the first five or ten years of his merchant navy career off-time cavorting with uneducated brown-skinned girls in seamen's bars and on the beaches in little-frequented parts of the world and he'd had the option just to marry one of them and base himself there, but, instead, he'd gone with convention.

The skinny guard appeared. "Consul," he said.

"What?" said Thompson.

"Consul," repeated the guard. "American consul."

"I'm British," hissed Thompson as he got up. He knew the guard hated him and just wanted to annoy him. He followed the guard out of the cell and down the corridor. What the hell did the consul want now.

Maggie was staring into her Chinese tea pot and slowly picking up the strainer when Thompson burst in.

"Where is he?" he demanded.

"You should know, shouldn't you," she said. Her pet boy had moved out of the other room into the doorway. Thompson was aware that he was there but didn't look at him.

"I called it off," said Thompson.

"You don't call off those people," she said. "They think it's bad for their reputation. Potential clients think they backed out. They don't want to have to try to explain that their former client changed his mind. Who changes his mind about something like that." She turned her little black eyes onto him. "Don't worry. Nothing can be proved. There is no evidence. There is no body. A little girl just disappeared. It's my fault. I should have been stronger with the sergeant. Why didn't you find someone to shoot the sergeant?"

"I didn't find anyone to do anything," said Thompson, sweating.

"Yes, you did," she replied. "But do you know what? You just wasted your money and maybe you killed your radio officer. Who knows what the sergeant may do now. He is furious. He may have your radio officer killed in jail. He may just find another girl to say he raped her and make up all the evidence. Why did you make everything so complicated. Time is getting on. You cannot treat us Asians as your playthings anymore. And the journalist is gone isn't she. And so it was a waste of time. And another one won't come. Thompson, you are a fool, the biggest fool I ever met in my life and I was in China dealing with officials who thought you could treat ballet like a factory. I have met some fools, yes I have. But you are the biggest."

"What can I do?" said Thompson.

"Do nothing Captain," she said. "Like you should have done in the first place. Just go away." Thompson turned and pulled aside the curtain over the doorway, letting in the blinding sunlight and stood there, squinting.

What do I care? he thought. "Just another bar girl. He'd had a sailor who'd murdered one once himself and he hadn't found out until they were at sea and the company didn't want to know. He let the curtain flap go on his way out and it swooshed back and forth behind him.

He wanted a drink with Warren, his protégé. He wanted some comfort. He wanted... his wife? She would just look at all this practically. "You were trying to help your friend?" she would say. I was, thought Thompson. I was trying to help my friend. He thought if he just told himself that the girl had gone away then it would all be O.K. He could live with himself.

He wandered away down the street. He would go back to the ship. He didn't want to be alone.

Roxanne was lying on her side in bed, looking at the sleeping chief engineer's son. It was still daytime and the sunlight was streaming through the windows and giving his face a glow. She smiled at him.

Suddenly, the door burst open and Warren stood there. She screamed and clutched the sheet to her breasts while Warren turned white. "No wonder the woman on the desk looked pale," he said.

"Warren, it's only...," she started.

"Get up you soft Southern bastard," he said to the chief engineer's son. Something puzzled him though. The chief's son did not look frightened, just mildly perturbed.

"I'd rather not, I've got no clothes on," he said. Warren was trying to think of something to say to that when Roxanne interrupted.

"It's not what you think Warren," she said, "I don't love him." Warren's jaw was hanging open.

"How does that make it better," he said. Roxanne's face flushed.

"What about you. I've seen you, leering at all those Asian girls and the journalist," she said. I bet you went there didn't you." Warren stared at her for a moment and then he turned to the chief engineer's son. "Get up," he said. The chief engineer's son sighed and then rose from the bed. Warren walked over to him. No sooner had he raised his fist than the chief engineer's son had caught it and twisted his arm up behind his back. Warren screamed.

"Warren!" said Roxanne. She started to hit the chief engineer's son, and the chief engineer's son let him go.

"What do you want?" he said to her, half in amusement, half in frustration. "You want him.

You already had him. I didn't chase you, you chased me."

"That's not true Warren," said Roxanne, turning to face her fiancé.

"Listen Warren," said the chief engineer's son to his victim, who was rubbing his arm. "Do yourself a favour. Marry her. If you're ever unfaithful to her, she can hardly complain can she."

"You bastard," said Roxanne.

He stepped forwards and gave Warren a little shove and Warren slunk away. "Don't be embarrassed that you got cooled off by a soft Southerner," he said. You tried to avenge yourself. That's the main thing." He walked past him and out of the door, still naked.

Warren looked at Roxanne with pain in his eyes. "Does it hurt Warren?" she said. "I mean the arm." He said nothing. "You shouldn't have brought me here to this terrible place," she said.

"The captain told me not to," said Warren. "I didn't listen."

"You should have listened Warren," she said. She looked at him sympathetically. "Come here," she said. He went over to the bed and she pulled his head down onto her chest. "Our first big fight Warren." she said.

"Yeah," said Warren. He raised his head. "I can't trust you now can I?" he said.

"You can trust me more," she replied. "I was unfaithful to you but I'm still with you. You get someone else and she is going to get an itch while you are at sea and go with someone and fall in love with him."

"That is some weird feminist logic," said Warren.

"Feminine not feminist," said Roxanne. He was surprised that she knew the difference. He supposed it had been hanging out with the lady journalist.

"I'm supposed to be at work," said Warren.

"Your surrogate father won't care," she replied.

"Why didn't I listen to him?" he said.

"Don't think about it Warren," she told him.

"Roxanne," he said. "I never went with any of those girls."

"Yeah, well don't start," she said. "I don't want a disease."

"But why did you believe I did?" he asked her.

"Everyone kind of told me without saying so," she said.

"It's not true," he replied.

"O.K. O.K," she said. "I suppose you could if you wanted to now," she said. "Couldn't you. I suppose it would only be fair."

"I don't want to," he said. Roxanne hugged him tightly. He was either pathetic or loveable, she told herself.

In the next room, the chief engineer's son lay on his bed and thought that this whole ships thing was insane. His father had always sat at the kitchen table like a zombie when he got home. He'd always assumed that he was just miserable but now he knew the truth, he was round the twist. They all were. Even their women.

There was something he had to deal with before he went, and he was looking forward to it. He was sure all his skills would be called into play but that was cool. He admired his biceps and flexed them.

Through the thin partition he could hear Warren sobbing and her cooing. He would have laughed but for the fact that they would have been able to hear him through the partition and he thought he really had caused them enough humiliation for one day.

"So who told Warren that his girl was sleeping with the chief's son?" asked Thompson.

"Phil," suggested the second mate, a fifty-year-old alcoholic with a shrew-like face. "He hates the chief."

"Not Phil's style," said Thompson. "And he won't like you suggesting it."

"You asked?" said the second mate. Then after a pause, "You're not going to tell him are you?"

Thompson just smiled. "It's not fair. You asked," whined the second mate.

"I won't tell him," said Thompson. He felt the second mate's sigh of relief. He wondered why everyone was terrified of Phil. So far as he was concerned it was good for discipline to have him on board. Everyone was just that little bit quieter.

The radio officer's cell was damp and humid and full of natives. He sweated yet still huddled in the blanket which was now his only possession. Some of the others in the cell had been giving him a hard time.

His problem was he didn't have the kind of friendly open face which might have led to him getting away with sitting in there with them and being regarded as an entertaining oddity. Warren could have probably managed it, but he looked guilty. He, himself, looked like the sort of man who might force himself on an underage girl even though he hadn't.

The cell boss was tolerating him because, thought the radio officer, he'd been told to. The other Europeans and the Americans were down the other end of the alleyway. They were mostly in for the same thing, but they'd been there a long time.

He looked at the sewage bucket where the cell boss had put his letter from his mother after he, himself, had finished reading it with some help from one of his followers. He wondered what she'd said. He'd never cared what she thought but now he found he did. I broke my mother's heart, he said to himself.

The cell boss stood up and stretched and looked over at him. The radio officer wondered if it was going to come now. He knew, through the prison grapevine, that the crew had tried to protect Roly, and he'd still been stabbed. No one was even trying to protect him.

The man walked over to him and tickled him under the chin and flashed a gold-toothed smile, and he shrank back, but then the man went and pulled himself up on the window bars so that he could see into the courtyard.

This is intolerable, thought the radio officer. Where is the consul. He didn't know why he'd suddenly thought of such an outdated word as intolerable. He wondered if he was losing his mind.

The sergeant was speaking to the head guard outside the cell block. The sergeant was furious that his witness and victim had disappeared. He could not believe that the radio officer did not in some way organise it. He'd already braced Thompson who shrugged and said offhandedly, "I know nothing Sergeant, I thought you had total control of this little town."

Soon, thought the sergeant, people would be laughing at him in the street. This man had already made a fool of him in front of his men once.

"Tell the cell boss to pick one man who is never going to get out and has a family he wants taken care of," he said to the head guard. The head guard sighed.

"It's not that simple, he's a foreigner," he said.

"You will be the man who runs the prison where even foreigners are not safe," said the sergeant. "That is something to be proud of. Imagine that, all the foreigners scared of you."

"No one will know me," said the guard.

"You will be on television," said the sergeant, "all over the world."

"Because I failed at my job," said the head guard.

"No one cares about him," said the sergeant. The guard still seemed reluctant. "Five thousand U.S. for you," said the sergeant finally.

"My nephew wants a job in the police," said the guard.

"O.K.," said the sergeant.

"And my mistress, secretary," said the guard.

"We don't have a secretary," said the sergeant.

"Then you need one," said the guard. The sergeant sighed.

"O.K., I'll run it past headquarters, he said. The guard looked doubtful. "Listen, I'll try," the sergeant continued.

Ten minutes later and the cell boss was called over to the bars. A minor guard whispered something, and the cell boss turned to the radio officer and smiled. The radio officer leapt to the bars, screaming, "Don't leave me in here," but the guard was already walking away, and the cell boss was beckoning one of his younger followers to get up.

Despatching the body home was a messy affair. The company reluctantly agreed to pay. Even for a company as evil as theirs, there could such a thing as bad publicity and as it was on television, refusing to pay the costs while the grieving mother cried her eyes out in front of the world was not good for business. Terry just took the whole affair as part and parcel of daily life. The chairman fumed. The chubby public schoolboys at his club were already snickering behind their copies of the Times.

Thompson watched with the agent as the coffin was loaded into the plane. The consul had looked horrified at their suggestion that they drape the red ensign over it.

"This is all good," the consul whispered to Thompson.

"What are you talking about," Thompson replied indignantly.

"Sorry captain, but if you were a devious official like me and not a plain-minded thug you would appreciate how this is good." He looked directly at Thompson. "Long term," he said.

"Maybe even short term." He paused. "Captain," he said smiling, "You didn't care about this one."

"I never said that," said Thompson. "I care about all my crew."

"Killed that little girl for nothing didn't you," said the consul.

"I didn't kill anyone," said Thompson too quickly.

"Killed, had killed, what's the difference," said the consul. Thompson was about to interject, but the consul carried on. "Shame they cut him up so badly. Makes an open casket difficult and his mother is a strict Roman Catholic."

"Will you just shut up," said Thompson. "Please just shut up. Go back to your ladyboy. You're no use here. This one's dead."

"This one is dead," said the consul, "but the other one is very much alive isn't he." He strode off in the direction of the hanger through which they'd been brought out onto the tarmac.

The consul sat surrounded by his diplomatic papers. "At last a chance to prove myself," he said quietly.

There was a little tap on the door and he opened it, and a local official slid in and sat in the chair in front of his desk, his cheap suit crumpling.

He hunched over and smiled. The consul swung round him and sat in his own swivel chair and pushed himself gently in a little arc.

"It looks terrible you know," he said. The local official opened his mouth to speak, but the consul waved his hand to silence him before he could start. "He was innocent until proven guilty," he said. The local official pursed his lips and the consul continued. "What we're looking for is a gesture," he continued.

"Your own government...," began the local official. The consul waved his hand again.

"We have a new government," he said. "A business friendly government."

"One which does not care about the environment," suggested the official.

"Our last government didn't care about the environment either, it was just rather more fashionable. Our prime minister," he paused, "new prime minister," he said, "will be visiting on a goodwill visit. He is touring South East Asia." The official was surprised. "This talk is behind the scenes," continued the consul.

"You haven't any authorisation from your Embassy or the British Foreign Office for these discussions have you?" said the official

"I do not," said the consul with a little smile. "This is not an official discussion. I merely suggest that you go to your boss and suggest that he suggests it to your president. There is no downside, only an upside. Your people don't really care about the spill. The next typhoon will pick all that damaged environment up and dump it somewhere else. You will appear to be a politically astute genius. Your boss will claim all the credit but will still look favourably upon you." The official pondered this. "That's all," said the consul. The official suddenly realised that he was being dismissed and got up. He shot the consul one last look at the door on his way out and then left.

The other prisoners whistled at the consul's ladyboy who sat on the horrible plastic seats while the consul waited for Roly at the partitioned cubicle. She smiled flirtatiously and crossed her legs.

The consul smiled at Roly as he walked up. Roly noticed the ladyboy. "Did you really have to bring him," he said with a sigh. "I can't believe the Foreign Office doesn't fire you."

"Lucky for you they didn't, and, in any case, they are not allowed to discriminate on the basis of gender, sexuality etc..." replied the consul.

"All the same, I think you can forget about Washington," said Roly.

"Who wants to eat canapés with Mid-Western congressmen anyway. I have my eye on Latin America after this," said the consul.

"I bet you do," said Roly.

"You are not looking well," said the consul. "Even worse than usual I mean."

"Very sensitive," replied Roly. "Worms." The consul recoiled in horror then recovered himself.

"We can either use that or not," he said thoughtfully. "We don't want to embarrass them."

"They are not going to let me out because I have worms," said Roly.

"I am working on a new angle," said the Consul.

"Yeah, yeah," said Roly.

"This is different," said the consul. "The only people who might screw this up are our own side."

"You mean the Guardian readers?" said Roly.

"Sort of," said the consul. "Such a shame you aren't a refugee or a terrorist or female or something. I'd have had you out months ago."

"We've been through that," said Roly.

"Yes, well listen. It's a lot more hopeful now. A lot more. What are you going to do about your worms?" he said.

"No medical treatment in here," said Roly, "apart from sewing up knife wounds."

"I will bring some medicine," said the consul. "Actually, I'm busy." He noticed Roly's rolled eyes. "Busy on your case," he said hastily. "Popsy will bring it."

"Please don't tell me you call him Popsy," said Roly. The consul got up.

"Why, don't you think it's a nice name?" he said. "Listen, seriously, hang in there. I've achieved nothing in my life. I glided through school with minimal effort. I played pretend soldiers for a few years. I am determined to have at least one success."

"I'm touched," said Roly. "My wife..."

"No nothing," replied the consul flatly. "Well, TTFN."

"This is all a big joke to you isn't it," said Roly. The consul leaned in towards the partition.

"No, it isn't," he said. "You will kiss me on the steps, out in the open air, soon."

Thompson lay in bed with his mama-san. She had wasted no time in reclaiming her place now that the lady journalist had left. "Your boy dead," she said.

"Yes, him dead," replied Thompson.

"Girl disappeared," she said.

"I didn't kill her," said Thompson slowly and deliberately.

"She bad girl, no problem," said the mama-san.

"I didn't kill her," Thompson repeated.

"Soon big trouble your boat," she told him.

"What do you mean?" he asked indignantly. "What big trouble?" He raised himself and looked down at her. "Do you mean Warren and the chief engineer's son?"

"Chief engineer's son, no Warren," she said cryptically.

"Tell me," he said.

"I no talker," she replied. "I no tell things police or captains." Thompson's face flushed and he laid back down in the sagging bed. "Big trouble your ship," she repeated. He fumed silently.

"Warren," said Thompson. "What's going on. I don't want any repeat of that fight. You were in the right; he was in the wrong; he's tougher than you are; he won; that's the end of it, you understand.

And by the way, you're a disgrace to the merchant navy," he added.

"It were Roxanne's fault anyway," said Warren.

"Was, Warren," said Thompson, "was, please don't copy her speech patterns. Anyway, that is a very sensible view. You're obviously not quite the blinded lovesick, little, puppy I took you for."

"Eh, thanks," said Warren.

"So, there's going to be no repeat performance," said Thompson.

"Repeat performance of my getting my arm nearly twisted out of its socket," said Warren. "I don't think so."

"So what else is going on with the chief engineer's son?" asked Thompson.

"I don't know," said Warren.

"That is most unsatisfactory Warren," said Thompson.

The agent appeared and signified to Thompson that he wanted to speak to him alone. Thompson shrugged and threaded his way through the pipelines and hatches. The agent was smiling, but that meant nothing. These people always smiled.

When he got up close, Thompson could see in the other man's eyes that there was something worrying him. He waited for him to speak.

"Don't leave the ship alone Captain," he said. "Maybe better not to leave the ship at all." Thompson waited for an explanation. "The sergeant," said the agent. Thompson snorted.

"He's already got one Englishman killed, you think he can get away with killing another?" he asked. The agent looked confused.

"Why not, you got away with killing that girl?" he replied.

"I didn't kill her, she disappeared," said Thompson.

"You might disappear," said the agent. "And anyone with you. You see the danger." Thompson thought about it.

"Yeah," he said.

"You should go home," said the agent.

"I want the thing with Roly finished first," said Thompson.

"You might wait thirty years," replied the agent.

"I was onto the consul, something might be happening," said Thompson. The agent looked surprised.

"Really?" he said. He shrugged and went to leave and then turned around again. He saw Warren watching them. "Remember, your crew too, not just you. Be safe Captain," he said.

"I'll try," said Thompson.

Warren appeared at his side. "Everything all right Captain?" he asked him.

"Yeah Warren. Just another day in paradise," said Thompson.

Thompson had always been stubborn and he wouldn't listen. Thus he found himself being braced by the sergeant when he left his mama-san's the next night. The sergeant had him up against a wall with a knife against his throat. Thompson's head hurt where it had been banged against the concrete.

"I know you had that girl killed," said the sergeant. "I even know who did it, I just can't prove it, and there's the killer's relatives involved. Powerful people, lucky for you."

"Yeah, well, the agent and the consul know you've been threatening my life, so if something happens, questions will be asked. You can't keep killing foreigners. If it weren't for the fact that the media considered him to be a paedophile, they'd have kicked up a bigger fuss about that."

"I don't need your permission Captain," said the sergeant.

"Listen, Sergeant, you've got it made. You run this town. You've got a government job on top of all the illegal money. Why do you want to stir it up? If you'd just left it all alone, none of this would have happened," said Thompson.

"He humiliated me," the sergeant hissed.

"By refusing to pay a bribe. Big deal," said Thompson. "Listen, I really don't care what you do with me. My daughter killed herself and I think I was too blame. Imagine that Sergeant. Imagine your daughter killing herself and you having to live the rest of your life blaming yourself."

The sergeant thought of his little catholic schoolgirl princess. "You should be afraid for yourself," he said trying to get the conversation back on track.

"Go ahead Sergeant," invited Thompson. "Stick the knife in." He grabbed the sergeant's wrists and began pulling him in, the tip of the knife just piercing the skin. The sergeant's veins bulged as he fought the desire to just let go but then he suddenly pulled away and stared at Thompson in frustration.

Thompson just looked at him pitifully.

The ambassador was fuming and trying to give the consul a hard time but he had such polite public-school manners that it wasn't going very well. "I've tolerated your insolence...," he said, only to be cut off by the consul's giggling.

"I was in the Army," said the consul, "and you're speaking to me as if I were some naughty fourth-former." The ambassador reddened.

"And that, that thing," he said.

"You can't fire me over Popsy," said the consul. "In fact, you can't fire me over anything because, if you do, I'll say you fired me over Popsy." The ambassador fumed even more. "Why do you care anyway?" said the consul. "You'll look good. You might get back to Europe and your classical concerts and soirees. You can have all the credit."

"You went behind my back," insisted the ambassador.

"So, I've been going in front of you for months and achieved nothing. I can't believe you're going to spoil this just because you didn't come up with the idea."

"I'm not spoiling anything," said the ambassador, irritated beyond measure.

"If this is going to go on, may I smoke?" asked the consul.

"Of course you may not smoke," said the ambassador. "Your irreverent attitude is maddening." They sat there in silence for a few moments, then the ambassador flipped his head in the direction of the door, and the consul rose and waited for the ambassador to offer to shake hands. The ambassador merely looked impatient, so the consul turned and went.

Popsy was waiting for him out in the open air, attracting admiring looks and comments from the capital's more open-minded denizens. "All good Popsy," said the consul. "All good. I consider myself to be the Machiavelli of the tropics." Popsy looked confused. "Not familiar with Machiavelli in ladyboy circles?" asked the consul. "Never mind. You're pretty enough that that sort of thing doesn't matter." He pinched her cheek gently.

The lady journalist sat in her editor's office in London. The editor shuffled some papers which he held in his hand and looked down his nose at her through his little John Lennon glasses. "So, you missed it," he said.

"I didn't miss it," she replied. "I was all over it. I told you I couldn't push for the captain because of the paedophile case."

"Oh really," said the editor. "We're under pressure to push against as many high profile non-political paedophiles as we can to take the heat of the government ones. This wasn't a decision for you. And the human interest angle with the poor old captain..."

"Which one?" she said.

"The one in jail of course," he replied.

"I didn't think you'd care," she said.

"Of course I don't care," said the editor. "I can't believe you blew an exclusive like this." He shook his head in amazement. The lady journalist usually connived to display cleavage or flash her legs in situations like this. but the editor was notorious for being immune to such blandishments.

"I have all my notes," she said.

"Yes, but you're not there while it's all happening are you," said the editor with irritation. "What's it like out there?" he asked suddenly. He himself had risen to the top through political machinations, he'd never been much of an on the spot reporter.

"They're all lunatics," she said. "The captains are the worst."

"Both of them?" asked the editor.

"Both of them," she said emphatically. She considered her options. "I could go back," she said.

"Maybe I should send someone else," said the editor. "You managed to come back without even mentioning any of this. Why should I send you again?"

"I'm a woman, that confuses those seamen," she replied.

"I thought seamen knew women very well," said the editor.

"Only hookers," she replied. "Faced with a woman who isn't, they're confused and easily manipulated."

"You're so cynical," he said.

"And I know the kingpin," she said.

"The captain in jail?" asked the editor.

"The other one," she said. "The one in jail is just the company's pawn." The editor looked sceptical. "I slept with him," she continued. The editor shrugged. "I had an affair with him," she said.

The editor sighed.

"Tell the travel department to book you a ticket," he said. "And if you come back without a brilliant story, you're fired."

The chief engineer's son spun and kicked and twisted in the hotel courtyard. Roxanne watched him from her bedroom window. He glistened with sweat and she sank her chin in her hands in adoration. Now he got out some kind of martial arts toy and began flicking it at a post. It seemed to make a very loud crack when it hit. Suddenly he looked up, right into her face, and she withdrew into the room embarrassed

The chief engineer's son smiled. He knew he could go back there whenever he liked but he didn't like. Let that Warren have her. He didn't want her anyway. Once he got her back home, she would start embarrassing him in front of his friends with her naivety and gaucheness.

He flexed his muscles and admired his biceps. He'd been exercising for an hour and he wasn't even slightly tired. He was going to make mincemeat of this guy. "I train for eight weeks to make it this easy," he remembered some boxer saying after he'd knocked out his opponent in ten seconds, leaving the audience unsure whether to be pleased by his display, or disappointed because their tickets had cost them ten dollars per second of entertainment.

Something had to be done, and he was the man to do it. He remembered his uncles' instructions. Kick here, kick there: street fighters.

Sometimes, he felt the strength and confidence flow through him and asked himself whether his father was really his father. How could a father and son be so different. But then, people said that they saw the similarities: The little cleft in the chin; the nose. The only person who would know for sure was his mother, and this wasn't the sort of question a son could ask his mother. Still, whatever; his father had put food on the table for thirty years and that entitled him to some loyalty.

Just the timing now. That was all. He had his ticket to go home soon. Sometime before that, obviously, and he had to decided where. It had to be in front of his shipmates, a public humiliation.

He pounded the bag he'd rigged up and looked slyly up at Roxanne's window. He couldn't see her but he thought she was watching from the shadows. He smiled.

The prison governor was being berated by an official from the president's office. "Idiot!" the man was screaming. "Fool!" The governor felt that he was being treated unfairly.

"The Government normally likes foreigners to be humiliated," he said. "To discourage the others."

"Worms," screamed the official. "He has worms! Do you realise how bad that makes us look? "Here we are, the entire country, trying to dispel these third-world images the westerners have of us, and you go personally trying to reinforce them."

"I didn't give him worms, he just caught them," said the governor.

"Because you didn't look after him," said the official. "Is there anything else I'm going to find out when I see him?" he asked. The governor reddened and shrank back into his chair.

"He was stabbed," he said. "But he is O.K. now," he added hastily. The official's eyes bulged. "Foreigners get stabbed all the time. No one cares," pleaded the governor.

"Ah," said the official, "so your defence is that you've shown no more than your customary incompetence. You'll be lucky if the president doesn't have you thrown into jail yourself." The governor knew this was all unfair. He'd pleaded for a dedicated wing for foreigners, but this had been denied by the central government over and over again. "Show him in," said the official to a minion at his side.

An emaciated Roly was brought into the room in chains. The official looked down at his ankles shuffling along and seemed ready to burst with fury. He only restrained himself so they appeared united in front of the foreigner.

"Captain, I am delighted to meet you," he said, "such a shame it's under these unfortunate circumstances. Please take a seat." He indicated the swivel chair in which the governor was sitting and the governor hastily vacated it. "All these misunderstandings are soon to be over," the official continued, soothingly.

Roly's wife was aghast. Her sons were pestering her while she tried to listen to the man on the other end of the phone. "But I don't understand," she said. "I thought..." She was quiet for a moment. Then she said, "Yes, yes, O.K." She put the phone down and looked at it with some irritation.

"Mum," said the older son. She didn't answer. "Mum," he said more loudly.

"Is it about Dad?" said the younger one?"

"He's not coming home is he?" asked the older one.

"Shut up," she said. The younger one looked at the floor, and the older one shrank back. "Unbelievable," she said. "Just when I have everything planned." She went over to the French windows and peered out at the garden, her pride and joy. All that love she'd put into it, she thought: Roly's money but her love. She turned to her sons. "Leave me alone," she said. They watched her as she turned and went up the stairs. The life insurance, she thought.

The lady journalist got off the plane and went through immigration. The immigration officer looked at her previous stamp and appeared puzzled. "So soon?" he said.

"I love your country so much," she told him. "The friendly people, the lovely beaches, I just couldn't stay away." British humour was wasted on the official. He stamped her passport with a flourish, and she was irritated to see that he'd placed his stamp right in the middle of a new page instead of squeezing it into another. The more third world the country, the more immigration officials were prone to do that, she thought. She picked up her passport and put it in her carry on bag and went out. She had no hold luggage.

The ride into the little town was too familiar. There was absolutely nothing that interested her. Thousands of poorly tuned two-strokes and shacks selling rice and chicken were no longer quaint, just tiresome.

She'd been a fool to leave last time and she had to make this a success. She needed to get Thompson back on her side first. That was the main thing. She had been right when she was with the editor. Thompson was the key.

The driver overcharged her but she couldn't be bothered to argue. She stood outside the same hotel and went inside and checked in. "Any of them still here?" she asked the clerk.

"Young girl and chief engineer's son," said the clerk. She sighed. Didn't that girl ever learn.

"Captain around?" she asked.

"Captain at seamen's club," said the clerk. She asked for her old room and went upstairs. As soon as she was out of sight, the receptionist rang the sergeant.

Thompson was taking coffee with the mama-san in her bar. The bar always looked so terrible in daylight. It was amazing how dim lighting and a few neon palm tree signs could transform such a dump into something so alluring. In daylight it was just revealed for what it was, a dusty watering-hole. Thompson and the mama-san said little, just relaxed. Thompson was reading the International Herald Tribune which came free with the better of the daily newspapers available in town, and the mama-san was sitting sphinx-like and sipping her drink.

Suddenly, the batwing doors swung open and the lady journalist stood there.

"Well, well," said Thompson. "Look who's back. Thought you'd given up on our little scene."

The lady journalist frowned. "Ask her to leave will you," she said.

"It's her place," said Thompson. The lady journalist stared at the mama-san, and the mama-san frowned and then got up and went into the back room. The lady journalist was still a customer, even if she did take liberties.

The lady journalist invited herself to a seat. "Things have changed," she said.

"Without your help," said Thompson. "When we needed you, you weren't here."

"I tried my hardest," she said. "It's not my fault if things moved on without me."

"And now you're back, like a vulture," Thompson replied. "You know I never should have trusted a journalist. My friend at school got in the papers once and he was quoted as saying, "And now it's down to some hard work for my O-Levels." He walked into their offices and said, "I didn't say that, how can you quote me?" and they said, "What are you going to do about it?" Made him look a right creep. No one at school spoke to him for a month. That's when I thought if journalists can lie like that, maybe they lie about everything. You could say that it wasn't important. But who decided what is important and what it's O.K. to lie about."

"Oh, don't be so childish," she said.

"I'm a seaman. I'm allowed to be childish. We're just big boys. Didn't someone say that to me not long ago. Who was that who said that to me?" He scratched his chin as if pondering the question.

"Enjoying yourself?" she said.

"I am actually," he replied. "Revenge is a dish best tasted cold."

"Best served cold, you moron," she said.

"I'm not a man of letters," he responded. "Or should I say woman of letters. Sorry. Lady of letters." She placed her handbag on the table in front of her and looked at him.

"Finished," she said.

"You've got a lovely body," he said. "Wouldn't mind seeing it again. But that'd make you a whore wouldn't it, exchanging that for information."

"I never slept with you for the story," she said. He snorted. "I slept with you because I was bored," she added.

"Well, I always did respect honesty," he replied.

"Good," she said. "Maybe we can get on."

"Get on? It's over with," said Thompson.

"He's not out yet," she retorted.

"Don't tell me you've come to complicate matters just to make it a better story," he said.

"Oh, don't be ridiculous," she said with undisguised irritation.

"But you got told off for coming back just a little bit early didn't you?" he said.

"Had your fun?" she asked him.

"I suppose I have," he said.

The chief engineer's son stood in the bright sunshine and looked at the rust-streaked hull of his father's ship. "What a dump," he thought once more. How could his father spend his whole life tramping around the world on such things. He sighed. He didn't understand.

He'd been waiting for his moment in the whore bars but the second engineer hadn't come out for a while and time was getting on. Soon, he'd have to be going home and he wanted the situation resolved.

He flexed his biceps and began the long tramp up the accommodation ladder. Some of the Filipinos were working at the manifold and their little eyes followed him through the slits in their coverings which they wore to stop their skin turning dark brown and making them look as if they were labourers which would lose them several social rankings when they went home.

He entered the accommodation block and threaded his way along the alleyways until he came to the officers' mess where he knew they'd all be taking their lunch.

As he came through the doorway, his father looked up at him and seemed puzzled. The son smiled at him and went over to Phil where he was tucking into his meal. He stood facing him. Phil took a while to notice him.

"What do you want?" he said when he did.

"Get up," said the chief engineer's son. Phil stared at him and went back to eating his dinner. The chief engineer's son kicked his chair. "I said get up," he repeated. Some cadets were sitting with Phil and they were riveted by the scene. Phil angrily rose and pushed his chair aside. "Outside," said the chief engineer's son. His father tried to say something, but his son shot him a glance and he gave up.

Suddenly, Phil seemed to look different. "What do you want?" he said but more quietly.

"I want to kick your head in, that's what I want," said the chief engineer's son. The cadets were looking at Phil with surprise and wondering why he hadn't already lashed out.

"I'm eating my dinner," said Phil.

"I don't care," said the chief engineer's son. "You like frightening my father, try and frighten me. Try it, because I'm going to kill you." Suddenly Phil's face flushed.

"A man is in jail because of his incompetence," he said.

"Yeah, I don't care," said the chief engineer's son. "Outside, or I'm going to do it in front of everyone." Phil didn't move and the chief engineer's son's fist shot out and broke his nose. Phil fell back with blood streaming all over him and made no attempt to get up when the chief engineer's son gave him a chance. The chief engineer's son booted him. "Get up, so I can finish this," he said. Phil's shipmates were confused. Why didn't Phil start fighting. He was taller than the chief engineer's son and season after season of rugby had formed a mass of muscle all over him. Some of them had spent years watching Phil intimidate all and sundry. If was as if the world had suddenly found out that the United States had no nuclear weapons and Pax Americana had all been founded on an illusion.

The chief engineer's son found his father's arms around him, and then Thompson barked from the doorway. "Get off this ship!" he said.

"He deserves it," said the chief engineer's son, spinning around.

"Get off this ship. I'm the captain of this vessel and I don't want you on board anymore and if you think you can try anything with me, go ahead. I'll wrap a spanner around your head long before you can get to the airport. I don't play fair like you do in your little dojo."

"Like you did with that girl you killed," said the chief engineer's son. Someone winced, and Thompson's face turned red with fury. He made a move towards the boy. "O.K. O.K. I'm going," the boy said, moving around Thompson and out the doorway.

Thompson pulled Phil up who shouted out, "A man is in jail because of this idiot!"

"Yeah, yeah," said Thompson, "calm down." He shot the chief engineer a look, and the chief engineer looked at the floor.

"My nose is broken," said Phil.

"Yeah, that'll take some explaining at home won't it," said Thompson. "I'll get in touch with the agent, and he'll have a doctor set it."

"Why didn't you hit him back?" said one of the cadets stupidly. Phil's hand shot out to his throat, but Thompson pulled his arm away.

"You weren't that keen to fight the chief's son were you Phil," he said. Phil flushed again. "Come on," said Thompson. "Ship's hospital. You're bleeding everywhere."

They left, and the chief engineer found himself standing in the middle of the room, looking stupid. He looked around him. The cadets avoided his eyes. The other officers looked like they didn't know what to say.

"It were nae my fault," said the chief. They weren't clear whether he meant the incident which put Roly in jail or the fight. "It were nae my fault," he repeated. Someone wanted to say, "Don't sweat it, we're all happy to see Phil get a kicking," but thought better of it.

The chief slowly went back to his place and slid down into his seat. He looked around him again and then slumped and put his face in his hands.

The chief engineer's son and Roxanne were hauling their bags into the antiquated lift. Warren was stressed. "You're flying together," he whispered to her. The chief engineer's son waited patiently in the lift holding the button.

"Yes Warren, we're flying together, if you think I'm going through that airport on my own, you're mad."

"But with him," said Warren.

"Warren, if you can't trust me, we might as well say it's over," she said. Warren was flabbergasted by the unfairness of this. He thought of saying, how can I trust you but he didn't want it to be over. She looked at him as if waiting for confirmation. He couldn't believe he had to confirm this. Then she leant forward and kissed him.

"I'll walk down," he said.

He arrived just as they were dragging their suitcases out of the lift and took hers off her and went out through the glass doors to the waiting taxi. Thompson had refused to put the transfer on the bill and send the agent. He'd told them that they weren't his or the ship's responsibility and they had both caused him a lot of stress. There was also the fact that the chief engineer's son had publicly accused him of being a murderer.

The suitcases were in the boot, and Roxanne kissed him lightly on the cheek, and the chief engineer's son shrugged and the two of them got in the car and the driver took them away.

Warren watched the taxi disappearing around the corner and sagged. It was out of his hands. He sloped off down the road.

Roxanne was tense, to the amusement of the chief engineer's son. She looked sideways at him, and he looked straight ahead. "Well, say something," she said.

"What do you want me to say?" he asked.

"We can't just leave it like this," she answered.

"You said you wanted company on the flight home, and I decided to accompany you," he replied. She tensed some more.

"That second engineer has a broken nose," she said accusingly.

"I should think he does," replied the chief engineer's son, "I smashed him pretty hard."

"And you twisted Warren's arm," she said.

"You think I did that because I love you?" he said with a little smile. Roxanne was infuriated. This wasn't supposed to be how it went. She had just been condescending to Warren and now the chief engineer's son was being condescending to her.

"I didn't say that," she snapped.

"Stick with Warren," said the chief engineer's son. "How many guys his age have as good a job as he does where you come from? You can still see other guys on the side, he'll be away for most of the time."

"I don't see other people on the side when I'm going out with someone," she said. She was waiting for him to point out the lie to this, but he just smiled again. "I should have gone home on my own," she said.

"Listen, let's just be friends," he told her. She bit her lip in frustration.

"I should never have come here," she said.

Thompson was in the agent's office on the phone to the U.K. "You serious," he said. The agent and his staff were watching him like a hawk. "Yeah, I'm just a bit surprised that's all," he continued. "Nothing, not even a little bit of help and suddenly this." He paused to listen to the other person.

"Yeah, yeah," he said. "Politics, I understand." He put the phone down and looked at the agent. The agent was not looking very happy. He did not like it when things were going on and he didn't know everything. He was used to floundering foreigners who were reliant on him and pleading with him for information. If he were expecting Thompson to enlighten him, he was disappointed. Thompson simply stood up and walked out. He stood for a moment, squinting in the bright sunlight. He'd always disdained sunglasses and, anyway, the radio officer's mother still had his.

So, the long ordeal might finally be over.

A car pulled up and the consul and Popsy got out. Popsy stretched herself to her full six-foot height and flicked her hair back to reveal the Versace logo on her sunglasses, and the consul smiled at Thompson. "Didn't let you down, did I?" he said.

"He's not been declared innocent," said Thompson.

"Bloody hell," said the consul. "What more do you want. He isn't innocent anyway."

"His career will be over," said Thompson.

"What is it with you guys?" said the consul. "His career was over anyway. He's fifty-six. The company's probably already got some plan to replace him with an Indian on half the money."

"That's not the point," said Thompson.

"You just can't bear the fact that there's no crisis for you to be dealing with can you," accused the consul. "Make a new crisis. Shouldn't take you long." He walked over to Thompson who was looking idly at Popsy. "He wouldn't have lasted much longer," he said.

"Yeah, I know, she'll kill him off anyway," said Thompson. The counsel looked surprised.

"Do you mean his wife? My boss says she's over the moon," he said. Thompson snorted.

"She will be I suppose, having her name in the papers. She'll milk that for all it's worth."

"I just don't understand you," said the consul. You guys are just depressives. Enjoy life." He waved his hand in his ladyboy's direction. "Like me and Popsy."

"Popsy and I," said Thompson absent-mindedly. "What public school did you go to?"

The consul put his arm around Thompson's shoulder. "Capitano," he said, "it's all good." He paused and stepped back and looked directly at Thompson. "You're not still worried about the paedophile are you?" he said.

"Stop saying that," snapped Thompson. "He wasn't a paedophile."

"There was no way to save him," said the consul. "You have to understand that."

"Yeah, yeah, I know," said Thompson.

"I saved fifty per cent of your people," said the consul with a little laugh.

"Yeah, you did that," said Thompson.

The scene outside the jail was chaos. A British T.V. crew was trying to shoo the locals out of shot while they interviewed Roly's wife but they were very left-wing and thus so keen to not appear condescending to the natives that they were too quiet and were ignored.

Roly's wife was enjoying her moment in the spotlight. She'd spent fifty pounds having her hair done and had on a very nice dress, which unfortunately, was more for the English climate and, due to the heat and humidity, was now revealing sweat stains. The eldest of her sons stood at her side, looking very solemn.

"It's going to be so lovely to have him back," she said. The consul giggled, and Thompson's face turned purple with rage.

"How many times did you visit him while he was in jail?" he asked. Roly's wife's expression changed. She looked very cross, and the interviewer turned around to face Thompson. He was scenting a development.

Suddenly the son interjected with, "My mother is very tired, that will be all for now." By the time the interviewer had turned round again, both the son and Roly's wife were looking up the steps of the jail entrance and not at him, and he couldn't resume the interview.

A native official was rattling away in the local language to a local T.V. interviewer. The consul, who understood, giggled again. "He is preaching the word of the lord," he said to Thompson. "Forgiveness etc.., making them feel they are morally superior to us when really it's all about a trade deal so the corrupt oligarchy of which he is a part can make even more money with which to keep the poor oppressed,"

"Just how in the hell did you ever get this job?" asked Thompson.

"Family connections," said the consul.

Inside the prison, Roly was being briefed by the man from the embassy. "You've been treated marvellously," he was told.

"I was stabbed and starved," said Roly.

"You couldn't have been starved or you wouldn't have got worms would you," said the official as though he were speaking to a distressed child. "You must have had something to eat, because worms come in food. Remember, you're still not out of the country."

"Have you got me on an R.A.F. plane?" said Roly. The embassy official looked at him in amazement.

"You really must have lost your mind in here," he said. "Of course we haven't got you on an R.A.F. plane. We don't send R.A.F. planes for convicts. You're not a hostage who's been released. You're on a commercial flight."

"Is the Government paying?" asked Roly. The official was exasperated.

"You've just spent nine months in jail. What do you care?" he replied. "But yes, the Government is paying." He anticipated the next question. "Economy class," he said. He motioned to Roly to get up, and Roly shuffled to his feet.

The guards and the governor leading the way, the little party went down the miles of corridors to the exit. There were no personal possessions to return to him as in the films. They'd all been stolen.

Roly blinked in the sunlight and felt the heat burning him. He was aware that some strange, pale, woman was clasping him to her and then it dawned on him that this was his wife, and then some pompous sounding public schoolboy was making an announcement, and he realised that this was one of his sons although, for the moment, he couldn't remember which one.

He saw Thompson and slipped away from his wife and went over to him. They were pressed in on all sides by locals.

"You got me out then," he said.

"The consul did," replied Thompson.

"Only because you threatened him," said Roly. Thompson shrugged.

"I don't think so," he said. "What will you do now?"

"They are flying me straight to the U.K," said Roly.

"Yes but I mean what will you do long term?" Roly shrugged.

"Not going back to sea am I," he said. "No one is going to employ a captain who had a spill. The insurance wouldn't allow it anyway."

"That bitch," said Thompson, looking at Roly's wife.

"Who cares," said Roly. "If I hadn't have married her, I would have married someone just the same." The T.V. journalist stuck a microphone in Roly's face. The journalist was just about to begin speaking when Roly smiled and launched into his own speech.

"I am very grateful," he said, "to the Foreign Office for their constant support and efforts throughout my ordeal and I am very grateful for this magnanimous act upon the authority of the local government in giving me mercy." He looked at the British official who was standing next to the consul. The official looked slightly perturbed but; nevertheless, nodded.

"Bit mangled," whispered Roly in Thompson's ear, "but I think I got the gist of what I was supposed to say."

"Your flight is this evening," said the official. We will take you to the airport." Roly looked at Thompson.

"Guess this is it then," said Roly.

"The chief engineer's son beat Phil up," said Thompson. Warren's girlfriend slept with him."

"Who, Phil or the chief engineer's son?" asked Roly.

"The chief engineer's son," said Thompson. "Phil doesn't sleep with hookers. Not that she's a hooker. You know what I mean."

"Phil was bullying the chief eh?" said Roly. Thompson nodded. "It wasn't all his fault," Roly continued. "The company wouldn't send the spare parts." The official was getting impatient. Roly reluctantly got into the back of the Jaguar, and then the official got in, and Roly's wife and sons, and the car sped away."

Thompson looked after it, and the consul came and stood at his side. "All over," he said.

"Where's Popsy?" said Thompson.

"You kidding?" said the consul. "In front of the British T.V. cameras. Even I wouldn't push it that far." He smiled a sneaky little smile. "Why?" he said.

"Just wondering," said Thompson.

Thompson's mama-san raised her eyes when he walked in. Why did the place always seem so dusty, Thompson asked himself while the doors were open and the sunlight was streaming in. Once they had swung shut, the joint was returned to its customary gloom.

He sat down opposite her, and her pet boy slid away into the other room.

"Congratulations," she said. "Your friend is going home. I like him. He is a nice man."

"Not like me," said Roly.

"Not like you," she affirmed.

"He has already gone," said Thompson.

"You are alone again," she said. "The others are just your crew, they are not your friends."

"No they aren't," said Thompson.

"You'd like to start sleeping with me again," she said. Thompson shrugged. "Now your, whitey, blondie lady has gone," she continued.

"If it makes you feel any better, she wasn't a real blonde," said Thompson. "Anyway, you are a professional. You should take things like that in your stride."

"I could love you Thompson," she said.

"I'm too old and I don't have enough money to take care of you," he replied.

"Yeah, yeah, I know. Your bitch wife took it all," she said. "Maybe Thompson. I will think about it. Leave me alone for a while. You made a fool of me. Briefly, I was a captain's woman and then, as soon as you took up with her, I was a whore again." Thompson didn't know what to say. "Go on, go," she said. Thompson reluctantly got to his feet and went out into the bright sunlight again.

The consul's little red sports car was parked in the street and he went over and stood by it and in a few minutes, the consul and Popsy turned up.

"Just been sorting out some loose ends with the radio officer," said the consul cheerfully. "What's wrong with you. You look glum. You got what you wanted captain. Be happy as the song says." The consul's eyes shot to Thompson's mama-san's place. "Romantic troubles?" he asked.

"How can you always be so happy?" asked Thompson.

"People are as happy as they make up their minds to be. Abraham Lincoln," said the consul. He kissed Popsy on the cheek. Popsy was studying Thompson, perhaps evaluating him. "Your ship will leave soon?" asked the consul.

"Yeah," said Thompson. "The market's picked up. They're bringing out the laid-up ships. We've done some repairs. It's not been an entirely wasted time."

"You should live here," said the consul. "It'd suit you. Life is cheap. People will leave you alone. Perhaps you'd do best to get off the sergeant's patch though. Have you heard from Captain Roly?"

Roly's in a worse living hell than that jail was," said Thompson.

"So cynical," said the consul. He nodded to Popsy. "Get in," he said. "Must go," he told Thompson. "We have parties to attend, gin and tonics to drink, cigars to smoke. You understand."

"Yeah, have fun," said Thompson. The consul nodded. He climbed in and was about to drive away when Thompson stopped him.

"Eh, thank you," he said. The consul laughed.

"Well, that took some effort didn't it Captain," he said. "But I appreciate it. I was just doing my job though. I actually feel myself to be successful at something at last." He waved and they sped off.

Thompson looked after the little car and took a look around and wandered to the bus stop.

He wanted to be surrounded by people. He didn't want to be sitting in a taxi, isolated.

He took a long look at the street. How could it seem such fun at night, and so dusty and horrible in the daylight. He'd spent his life on this same street though it'd been in different countries, the whores had had slightly lighter or darker skin, the shopkeepers had been slightly friendlier or unfriendlier. How long could he go on. Forever.

The bus came and stopped but Thompson didn't get on. The driver sorted all the locals out and then looked at Thompson, shrugged, and drove off.

Thompson just stood there in the dust, alone and forlorn.

He went over to the bar opposite the mama-san's and sat down outside and waited for someone to serve him. He thought about going to Maggie's but the emotional effect if he were thrown out would be too much.

The proprietor's wife bought him a beer and he handed her the equivalent of five dollars and told her to keep the change. She looked confused and then went inside quickly with a broad smile on her face, before he had time to change his mind,

The pet boy appeared in front of the mama-san's place and then went inside, and then the mama-san appeared and stood looking at him. She frowned and then, seemingly reluctantly, waved him over.

"You're bringing shame to me, sitting there, like I won't look after my lover and best customer," she said.

She led him by hand inside the joint and straight through to the room in the back with the bed. She placed her hands on his cheeks and then kissed him on the lips.

"Sometimes, I do things for charity," she said. "Everyone wants to help poor little kids who are rolling around in the dirt, playing and laughing and yet who needs help the most Thompson, people like you, lonely British merchant seamen. My life's work."

"I'm in need of charity all right," said Thompson.

"Your wife's a fool," said the mama-san. "You're a decent man."

"I'm a thug and maybe a killer," he said.

"Life is not for judgements Thompson," she said. "God will do all the judging when we are dead."

She pushed him back onto the bed and lifted her dress over her head.

"I'm only thirty Thompson," she said, "and I know more than your wife who is probably sixty."

"You sure do," he replied.

26542729R00119

Printed in Poland
by Amazon Fulfillment
Poland Sp. z o.o., Wrocław